Bind

donalee Moulton

Print ISBNs

Amazon Print 9780228634089
Ingram Spark 9780228634096
Barnes & Noble 9780228634102
BWL Print 9780228634119

Copyright 2025 by donaleemoulton
Edited by Nancy M Bell
Cover Artist Pandora Designs

Dedication

For Aunt Trixie.
Who showed me the joy of a downward dog.

Acknowledgements

Bind is my third mystery. What I have learned writing, editing, publishing, and promoting three novels is that my work is not a solo endeavor. I am indebted to many people who support me, guide me, and, in the process, make me a better writer. I would like to thank a few of those many people here.

As *Bind* was emerging from child's pose and moving into a full warrior one, the book had several beta readers – people who were frank and kind. Their feedback was invaluable. Thank you to Sue MacLeod, Rusty St. John, Rand Gaynor, Linda Roberts, and Heather Marriott.

Two dear and skilled friends deserve a lifetime of thanks. Throughout the process of bringing *Bind* to the world, Cheryl Enman read, reread, edited, and proofread the book. Her patience and care are etched on every page. One day, she says, she'll even come to a yoga class with me.

With the launch of *Bind* comes the work of letting the world know. Lynn Bruce, whom I affectionately call CPO, my Chief Promotions Officer, did not wait for the official arrival of the book. Already in the works are readings, book fairs, bookstore signings and more. Lynn does come to a yoga class with me.

This book lives and breathes on digital bookshelves, actual nightstands, and in the hands of readers thanks to BWL Publishing. JD Shipton, VP and Supervising Editor, gently and effectively helped *Bind* become much more than words on a page. It's a book thanks to JD's work on my behalf. My appreciation to Nancy Bell, my editor, who was diligent and thoughtful. Both are appreciated.

I owe a debt of gratitude to BWL's publisher, Jude Pittman who has supported my work from the first words of my first book and continues to offer advice, insight, and suggestions – as well as opportunities to expand and grow as a writer. I am in your debt.

Bind exists in large part because I love yoga, and I have learned to love yoga because many teachers have taken the time to nurture what nestles within our hearts, our muscles, and our spirit. Two, in particular, have gone above and beyond. To Careen McNeil who has taught me to push myself – with joy. To Jane McCullough who has taught me to surrender – with gratitude. Thank you for this gift.

And last but never least, to Allan.

Table of Contents

Chapter 1.

OCTOBER POSES +

Focus: flexibility and alignment
Poses: binds
Goal: bird of paradise
Mantra: I find happiness from within. I share my happiness with others.
Mudra: Jala (thumb and little finger together)
Chakra: sacral
Activity: daily thoughts (handwritten)

The early morning sun glints off the Bedford Basin. It bathes the Asana Yoga Studio in warmth and light. Oak floors gleam. A bronze frog in full lotus smiles. There is stillness and serenity.

There is a hint of something else.

Kristi Yee does not sense anything but the tranquility she is about to shatter. The studio owner opens the double doors at 6:26 and steps inside. Quietly and respectfully. This is her second home (maybe even her first) and much more than a business, although it is that, too. The 35-five-year old takes a minute to breathe in peace, exhale gratitude. It is her morning ritual.

Now it is down to work. Within the next 30 minutes anywhere from five to fifteen yogis of all shapes, sizes, and commitment levels will descend on this space. They will twist, stretch, and hopefully, find a glimmer of inner calm. Kristi will help them on their journey. She does not know it now, but for Kristi and three of those participants, that journey will be unlike any they have ever been on before.

It's October 1st. Each month Kristi posts a list to guide the poses and activities the group will do over the next four weeks. After 14 years as a certified yoga instructor, Kristi has learned it is necessary to engage and inspire participants. To push and embrace them as they move forward, and sometimes, backward.

Kristi writes on the whiteboard the props her yogis will need for today's class: two blocks, one kneepad, one blanket. Soon she will add, at least mentally, nerves of steel. Binds are not easy. While physically they give you more leverage to get deeper into poses, they also require you to twist, contort, and reach, reach, reach.

Kristi picks up a plastic-lined basket filled with wristbands. Each band gets two drops of ylang ylang essential oil. Next Kristi reaches for an orange aromatherapy diffuser and heads out the door to the washroom. It's like entering an alien domain.

The sense of something else is stronger here.

Asana Yoga is located inside a gym, Vitality+. Members join the gym and can take yoga classes at no cost. Despite the financial and physical interconnection, the two worlds rarely meet. Gym goers grunt and sweat, look at themselves in the mirrors that line three of the gym's four walls. They pump and preen. The yoga participants, who usually walk quickly through the gym and breathe a sigh of relief when the studio doors shut gently behind them, move quietly through poses looking for balance and, ultimately, grace.

By the time Kristi is back in the studio, diffuser full of natural spring water and ten drops of rose oil, two of the group have arrived. They are reading the whiteboard. Kristi hears a quiet groan. Not everyone likes binds she tells herself but knows deep down (and really not all that deep) the groan has little to do with the monthly poses and everything to do with having to keep a journal no matter what Zen name you give it.

The three women say their good mornings and smile. By the time they all have their mats unfolded and props at the ready, three more participants have entered the studio. More groans can be heard around the whiteboard.

The final participant arrives with only a minute to spare. Shondra Aeron glides in wearing harem pants, a Mother Earth t-shirt, and a big smile. The group smiles back between warm-up stretches and breathwork. Everyone likes Shondra, but no one calls her that. To the group, she's Woo Woo. A reflexologist, reiki practitioner, and tarot card reader, Woo Woo is warmly seen by many in the group as a little ... well, you get it.

At 7:01, Kristi welcomes everyone and begins the class with a reflection. Participants, flat on their backs, breathe in/out, in/out. They set an intention. Today the intentions are predictable: strength, balance, flexibility.

That will change over the next several weeks.

The first bind is bound side angle, a relatively easy position until Kristi suggests they try lifting their extended foot. Several people stumble. Lexie falls. The next bind is Marichyasana A. It requires hamstring flexibility, hip mobility, and internally rotating the shoulder. It does not go over well.

Kristi moves the group to the floor, a signal life is about to get easier and the class will soon end. A few twists, then the group settles in for savasana. Kristi leads them through a yoga nidra. Scented bands are gently placed on each participant's wrist.

The Asana Yoga Studio glows with contentment.

After a few minutes, the yoga nidra ends. Kristi brings the group back to the present. "Wriggle your fingers and your toes. Stretch legs, arms overhead."

For the last movement, the class draws their knees into their chest.

Woo Woo breathes in contentment.

Charlene breathes a sigh of relief.

Honey farts.

Something lingers.

Participants are packing up. Blocks, blankets, and kneepads are returned to their proper places. The diffuser is turned off. The bronze frog continues to smile. Lexie raises her arm. Four other arms wave back. This is the ritual that follows yoga class: coffee and sweets.

Vitality+ is located inside a 12-storey office complex. On the ground floor, in addition to the gym, is a coffee shop and bakery. Here yoga participants gather to indulge for a few minutes. Kristi thinks it is because they want to carry what they experienced on the mat into their day. Deep down she knows a cobra pose cannot compete with a cappuccino and cinnamon roll. Charlene and Woo Woo are the first out the studio door. They head over to the café to snag a table. Honey and Kristi follow a few minutes later. Lexie is the last to leave. She takes a few seconds to look around the gym.

Nathan, a young man behind the main desk in the entranceway, waves. Lexie beams.

Charlene has taken over the corner section of the coffee shop with its overstuffed chairs and cushioned sofa. While the entire café is comfortable and welcoming, this is the best spot – in a quiet corner with an expansive view of the Bedford Basin. Charlene has a knack for claiming this territory. There is a look she gives that deters anyone from coming near. Lexie thinks all auditors learned this look in university: Facial Expressions 101 for Accounting Professionals.

By the time Lexie arrives with her latte and chocolate chip cookie, the group is debating the merits of doggy day care. There seems to be unanimous agreement that this activity is healthy for dogs. Then Charlene, who owns a Westie named Madoff, gives everyone a look. Discussion over.

"Tell us about this week's podcast," says Honey.

Lexie, a comedian for more than 20 years, started Punchlines in 2014. It's easier than stand-up and much more lucrative. In addition to free stuff, there are advertisements. All Lexie does is chat with guests who have some connection to the world of comedy. She hopes to give listeners an inside look at the often-unfunny life of comics. Sometimes she just phones it in.

"You'll like the show," Lexie says to Honey. "I'm interviewing Crystal Ball." She gets looks from everyone around the table and a few snickers. "She's a great-niece of Lucille Ball who once spent a summer at her house in LA."

"That's incredible," says Woo Woo.

Lexie knows it isn't.

Daily Thoughts – Lexie Hill
Friday, October 1st

Sharing her thoughts – especially with herself – does not come easily or naturally to Lexie Hill. Indeed, she's avoided doing this most of her life. But she's taking the yoga class, perhaps as a way to plumb for new comedic material, perhaps to offset what she tells herself is increasingly high blood pressure.

Or perhaps it's something else altogether.

No matter what her motivation, Lexie is all in (ish). For six months, she has turned up regularly for classes. She tries to follow instructions and commit to her practice. She also tries to do the damn monthly activity. Last month it was doing stretches first thing in the morning. Lexie would place her coffee about three feet in front of her, bend, and reach. She did this three times. Every morning for 30 days. Lexie believes this was in keeping with the spirit of the assigned monthly activity.

God, she misses September.

Yo.

I won't ask how you're doing. I know. You're doing okay. The podcast is going well – more than paying the bills, and CBC has invited you to do an episode of *The Debaters*. Life is good. Well, work is good, and you like your work. How many comedians can say that with a straight face.

The yoga practice is fun. Sorta. I'm getting better at triangle and plank. I can feel myself getting stronger and more flexible. One day I may even be able to do a malasana squat. If that never happens, I still have one helluva bit for my next act.

The group is okay. We go for coffee after class. Talk about the weather and our aches. Sometimes we talk current events. It sounds funny, but I feel like I'm getting to know them even though we don't open a vein and bleed. My kind of people.

I'm not sure how long I'm supposed to keep this daily thought running. I'll ask Kristi. In the meantime, I'll go make myself another coffee and extend my reach.

LH

PS I saw him today.

Chapter 2.

The gym reeks of sweat. It hits Kristi in the face (and her heart chakra) every time she walks through the front doors. This is early morning sweat, the worst kind. Only the truly fervent are up, dressed, and exuding moisture beads at this time of the day.

Kristi waves to her business partner, Jaxx Taylor, behind the front desk. There was a time the yoga instructor wanted more of a relationship with Jaxx. One that involved lips and other bits coming together. That time has passed. There is only so often someone can remind you what good friends you are before you take the hint.

Jaxx runs the gym, what Kristi calls the sweat shop, and handles the finances for Vitality+. Kristi operates the yoga studio and related activities. She also handles administration. They both do marketing, which amounts to little more than updating their Facebook page and leaving the rest to word of mouth. Seems to be working. Only five years old, the gym is a hit. There are more than 300 members and growing. It may be location. It may be the owners. Hell, it may even be the smell of sweat.

Once a week Kristi likes to do a deeper clean of the yoga studio. The maintenance crew mops, dusts, and sweeps every night, but there are nooks Kristi likes to scour, and she rearranges the props cupboard and the storage room in back where yoga mats and other items tend to tumble over each other as the week wears on. Organizing and cleaning is a form of meditation for Kristi. Or so she tells herself.

Kristi gets an old toothbrush from her cleaning supplies and hits the south side of the studio, farthest from the bay windows and the view of the basin. She dives in. When she's done, the wood paneling shimmers in the early morning sunlight and a small pile of dirt, from under the wainscotting, remains to be sucked up in the hand vac. Kristi smiles.

After that, she tackles the prop closet making sure mats are carefully aligned, so as not to tip or fall. Blankets are neatly piled on top of one another within easy reach. Chairs are stacked at the back, no longer in danger of spilling onto the floor or unwary toes.

Within the next 15 minutes, five yogis arrive, dragging mats and blocks and blankets and straps onto the floor of the studio. This is the fun part of class, the coming together, hellos and high expectations. Nothing hurts at this point; there is no reminder of bodily limitations.

As the participants unfurl mats, do a few cats and cows, and find child's pose (usually gingerly), Kristi places a foam block in front of each mat. Six more people arrive. Six more blocks. More hellos. Three more cats and cows.

Kristi leads the group in an opening meditation: temporal landmarks. Just as we use landmarks to position ourselves in space we use other landmarks – landmarks unique to us – to guide our lives. "Take a minute to see your life from 30,000 feet," Kristi says in a voice that is calm, resonant. Bhodi will try to replicate this later in the privacy of his condo.

"Focus on what you want to achieve in this life, small or large. Imminent or long term." Charlene starts a list. She mentally numbers it from one to five. She gets to three when Kristi says, "Think about your life goals. Slowly. Look at each goal and assess its value for you. For now." Charlene feels she has done the exercise incorrectly and starts her list again.

"We'll come back to temporal landmarks during savasana," Kristi says after a few minutes. "Now, blink your eyes open. Take in the space around you." Woo Woo glances at the ceiling, puts her hands in prayer position and moves them to her third eye. Lexie yawns.

The group moves from table to a vinyasa flow: plank, chaturanga, upward-facing dog, downward dog. This is familiar territory for everyone, albeit uncomfortable for most of them. It's also a harbinger of aches to come. Sure enough. Up next: lizard pose, utthan pristhasana. "Try saying that three times fast," Lexie thinks. Woo Woo silently wraps the syllables around her tongue. She giggles quietly.

Lizard pose is intended to open up the hips. A good start, Kristi says, for the binds to come later. It's a great way to stretch hamstrings and quadriceps, she adds. It can help reduce stress, improve focus, and release emotion. Bonnie, new to the group, thinks this is true. She wants to cry.

Bind of the day is Marichyasana A, a seated forward fold with one knee raised. It's doable, to some degree for everyone in the class. Kristi suggests taking it to the next level. "Try to touch your nose to your extended leg." Bhodi looks around to see if anyone can get as close to their leg as he can. Bonnie wipes away a tear making its way down her left cheek.

Tree pose, balance pose of the day, is a welcome relief. Some members nestle their foot against their ankle; others bring it to the calf. Bhodi brings his to the inner thigh. Lexie thinks he's a bit of a dick. She tries bringing her leg to her thigh. It falls down. She catches Bhodi grinning.

Kristi presciently (or perhaps just observantly) reminds everyone there is no right or wrong. "Listen to your body." But the sage advice is lost in an uproar from outside the studio. Kristi makes her way to the closed studio doors telling participants to move to the mat and child's pose. "Hold for a count of ten."

Then Kristi does something she has never done before during class. She leaves the room.

Child's pose is supposed to be a resting pose. Charlene thinks this is false advertising or whatever the yoga equivalent is. It's a simple enough pose in its description: knees are spread as wide as the mat, the tops of your feet are on the floor with big toes touching. Forehead comes to the floor. The bum rests on the heels. Problem is bums rarely rest on heels. Charlene crams a bolster between her buttocks and feet. Woo Woo leans back and envisions her glutes sitting on her heels. Archina King, another newcomer, thinks this may be the longest 10 seconds of her life.

Kristi is back in the room. There is still some noise from outside, but it is quieter now. "Let's move into savasana." There is a collective sigh of relief.

Bonnie nestles under a blanket thinking, "I didn't do all that badly."

Lexie looks toward the studio doors in anticipation.

Honey farts.

There is a bigger crowd today for coffee – seven participants. Charlene heads out the door quickly to lay claim to the café sofa and chairs. Just as quickly she's brought up short. A small crowd has collected around the front desk. It doesn't seem happy. At the center of the firestorm appears to be a man with a loud voice and the self-assurance that only money and position can bring.

"What are you going to do?" he demands.

Charlene walks by as slowly as she can, not wanting to miss a word but not wanting to look like a gawker. The gym's co-owner, Jaxx, tries to reassure the angry man everything possible will be done. Woo Woo comes up behind Charlene. She gawks. "What's going on?"

"I haven't got the faintest idea," says Charlene, "but whatever it is, it's not good."

The group finds out over coffee what is going on. At least what they know. Between Kristi's quick exit during class and the line of yogis leaving the studio, slowly, the group is able to piece together much of what has happened. One of the gym members (Bonnie thinks his name is Newhouse) has lost his watch. He contends it has been stolen from his locker. Apparently, it's an expensive watch.

"It would be," says Charlene. Her tone is even. There is no sarcasm or envy. Everyone looks at her.

"He reeks of money."

Everyone continues to look at her. "Auditor stuff. You get to know quickly who's going to push their weight around because they can. These guys always want to show the world what they're made of: money. Timex won't cut it."

"Well, this guy could buy a lot of Timexes," says Lexie. Her phone is in her hand. She reads from the screen. "If we have his name right, he's founder and CEO of Bluenose Developments, a construction company in Halifax. Says here the company is worth $26 million."

"And he's upset about a watch?" says Archina.

"He's upset because he got bested," says Charlene. Everyone looks at her. She's getting used to this. "Rich men don't like to lose at anything. They think it's a sign of weakness."

"He probably has a little dick," says Woo Woo. Everyone laughs. Except Kristi.

The coffee klatch is breaking up. Bonnie offers Archina a drive home. Honey heads to the cashier to order a sandwich for lunch later. Woo Woo walks outside and stands still. Charlene can't figure out if she's having a heart attack or meditating. Woo Woo walks toward the parking lot. Apparently not a heart attack.

Lexie heads back upstairs with Kristi. "Left my bag in the studio," she says by way of explanation. Kristi nods absently. She's clearly worried about something and that something has to be related to what's going on in the gym.

Kristi has reason to worry. When she and Lexie walk through the doors, the first thing they see are two uniformed police officers. A young woman and a younger man trying to control the yelling, the interruptions, and the gesticulating. Kristi walks toward the group. Jaxx waves her away. She keeps on walking. Lexie looks around the room anxiously. She spies the young man from earlier standing behind the front desk partially hidden by one of the police officers and Timex, as she's come to call the developer. Lexie breathes a sigh of relief. No longer even pretending to be uninterested, Lexie, too, walks toward the group.

The youngest cop, badge number 6841, is trying to get everyone to quiet down. Suddenly the sound of an evil clown pierces the air. Everyone turns. Lexie has her phone in her hand. "I use this sometimes on my podcast," she says. The female cop shoots her a look. Lexie thinks it may be gratitude.

In the silence that has suddenly descended, the female cop, badge number 6211, says, "Let me see if I've got this right." Timex opens his mouth to interject. 6211 holds up her hand. The hand says, "Go ahead, make my day."

Timex clamps his jaw shut. Not a happy camper. 6211 continues. "There is a watch missing. That watch belongs to Byron Newhouse." 6211 nods in the direction of the short, muscular man with his jaws clamped shut. He nods curtly. "The watch was last seen in Mr. Newhouse's locker. That locker does not appear to have been tampered with, but the watch is missing."

Newhouse nods. 6211 nods back. "Let's go look at this locker, Mr. Newhouse."

"I'll start a search of the gym in case the watch got mislaid somewhere," says Jaxx. 6211 nods approval.

Kristi follows behind Jaxx. It's not clear whether she wants to help in the search or confront her partner. That may be because it's unclear to Kristi herself.

Lexie heads directly for the front desk and the young man standing very still behind it. "Are you okay?" she asks. Nathan Young's face registers surprise, perhaps at the question, at the source of the question, or at the fact he hadn't asked himself the question before now.

"Stupid, stupid, stupid," Lexie says to herself. Out loud she offers this up by way of explanation, "That did not look like a good situation."

"Mr. Newhouse is pissed. Really pissed," Nathan says. "He thinks one of us stole his watch."

"He said that?" Lexie asks. She is both shocked and angry.

"He accused the staff. Jaxx said we would never do anything like that. Then he said it had to be one of the other members."

This seems to sit better with Lexie. "Perhaps he's just an ass."

For the first time Nathan smiles. He also seems to come back into his physical space.

He looks around as if aware of where he is, what he's doing, and whom he is talking with. He draws back slightly. "I'm sure Mr. Newhouse is just upset about his watch."

"Understandably," says Lexie trying for safer ground. "I'm sure it was a very nice watch."

"He said it was a paddock for Phillip or something like that."

"I'm sure it was a very nice watch," says Lexie. Again.

Stupid. Stupid. Stupid.

Daily Thoughts – Charlene Kurtz
Monday, October 4th

Charlene is a rule follower. It fits with her profession and her personality. It's in her nature to take the road well travelled and adhere to the posted speed limits. There is no doubt she will complete the monthly activity assigned by Kristi. She won't shirk from the task, make excuses for non-compliance, or try to find a loophole. She may grit her teeth.

Interesting day at the yoga studio. *Charlene thinks this incomplete sentence is in keeping with the spirit and intent of the assignment – to be natural, to flow. Charlene is pleased with herself.*

Some man created a scene because he lost his watch. In fairness, it was probably an expensive watch. In reality, he is likely a dick. *Auditors have their own special jargon.*

It really upset Kristi. She actually left class for a few minutes. I felt her walk by me and opened my eyes. I know we're not supposed to do this when we're in a resting pose, but I figured it's allowed since there is nothing restful about child's pose. Someday my heels might say hello to my ass, but that day is a long way away.

I think Kristi is worried about Jock or Jacket or Jackass, whatever his name is. He tried to brush her off when we were going for coffee, but I don't think she'll be brushed away for long. I do hope everything is okay. I'm enjoying my yoga.

I'm going to continue consulting. It offers me some extra spending money and gives me something to do. I'm finding the days as a retired auditor longer than I had expected. I know I don't garden or golf, but I had imagined fuller days and nights. Perhaps that will come. I've only been retired for six months.

I might try reflexology. Woo Woo has offered us a reduced rate. Could be interesting and Woo Woo is very nice. I wonder if I go to her place? It would certainly be interesting.

So that's three "interestings" in this daily thought. Wonder what that says about my originality? Then again, auditors don't need to be original. Come to think of it, neither do yoga practitioners.

Sincerely,

Charlene Kurtz

PS He left me another message yesterday.

Chapter 3.

Byron Newhouse is pissed. If you were to ask him, he'd tell you the damn gym is irresponsible and does not have proper security. To himself, in some inner recess, he might admit some responsibility. He routinely loses his locker key. His Nike cargo pants have a deep pocket and a small flap. Sometimes he puts the key in one, sometimes the other. It doesn't seem to matter. At least twice a week, the key goes missing. He has a second key he keeps in his car, so access to his locker has never been an issue.

Still, this is inconvenient. He is fond of his rose gold Nautilus 7010. Looks good against his tanned wrist, and it sends an important message. His father wouldn't get the message, but when he found out the price, he'd be impressed. Or mortified. Either way, Byron doesn't really care. This is the cost of doing business. This is the cost of being an important person in the community.

Now he'll have to wear his Omega Goldmaster. It's a statement watch, but it's no Patek Philippe. Byron feels annoyance run through his veins. If it's one thing operating a business has taught him though, it's rolling with the tide. There will be good days and bad days. Being an entrepreneur has also taught him the lemon thing. And there are lemonade possibilities here. Surely the gym is insured. He certainly is. He can inflate the price. He might get a brand new watch to replace his six-year-old Nautilus.

He'll also have an opportunity to impress his son, to show him how a real man moves in the world, taking control and exerting influence to get things done – in your favor. It's a message Christian seems reluctant to receive especially now with that girlfriend of his. Byron does not like her. Truth be told, he's not sure he likes his son when he's with that girl. It's hard for Byron to recognize him. To find common ground. Maybe it always has been hard.

Curious, though, about the watch. Someone could have found his key, but how would they know what locker it opened? Did they try every locker? Even if someone had the patience for that, the changeroom is not empty for long. It's a busy gym. It would have been suspicious for a guy, and almost impossible for a woman, to spend any time in the changeroom trying out a key in random locks without raising eyebrows.

That makes Byron wonder if he's been personally targeted, and that pisses him off more. Perhaps he should call his lawyer. At least he'd be getting some value for his monthly retainer. Byron reaches for the phone. Then it occurs to him. He may not have lost his key. Someone may have taken it. If that's the case, it's someone close to him. Someone very close.

Chapter 4.

Kristi barely notices the sun shimmering on the water of the Bedford Basin or the glowing oak floors. She steps over the bronze frog and moves to the window as she does every morning. Today, the movement is more perfunctory than profound. More routine than ritual. Kristi turns to face the room before she fully exhales gratitude.

By the time the first yogis arrive – Charlene and Honey – Kristi has the room set up, the aromatherapy diffuser spewing holy basil. It may be that Kristi picked this scent because of its calming properties, or it may have been the first one her hand touched when she reached absently into the carrying case. Kristi walks past the two regulars and continues out the door. Honey looks after her and tilts her head to the left. Then shrugs her shoulders. Kristi forgot to say hi.

The yoga instructor marches toward the front desk. She asks Nathan if he's seen Jaxx. Nathan points toward the office she shares with her business partner. Kristi continues her march. She's not sure this is a good idea. She doesn't want to fight. She particularly doesn't want to get into an argument in the moments before yoga class starts. But more than that, she doesn't want to wait any longer for answers. Jaxx has been evading her questions for months, and it has been much too long since they sat down and had a business meeting. They used to do this once a month over pasta from Il Ristorante and a nice merlot from Luckett's.

It's time. Kristi raises her shoulders then lowers them toward her spine. She tightens her jaw. She strides into the office. Her office.

Jaxx is on the phone. He waves hello.

Then he waves her away.

* * *

Ten yogis are in various stretches, twists, meditations, and yawns when Kristi walks back into the studio. She forces a smile, and the smile spreads of its own accord into her muscles, her bones, her heart. This is her sanctuary. She is at home here. The rawness she feels is still there, but it has moved to the edges now.

Today's bind is a yogi squat. One leg is extended; the other is bent. One arm goes under the bent leg; the other goes around the back until they meet. In theory. Lexie can't wait until this month is over, and it's only day three. Bhodi looks around the room to see if anyone else has completed the bind. Surprisingly, Honey seems to have easily

35

maintained the squat and the bind. Bonnie begins the countdown until she can come out of the contortion, which for her is a little squat and a hint of a bind.

Kristi takes this opportunity to explain the benefits of binds. "These poses allow muscles to release, relax, and open. You can go deeper. You can also focus on alignment and flexibility while building strength." She breathes in.

"Dear God," thinks Lexie, "there's more."

"If you make her stop," Bonnie says to her higher spirit, "I will give you my first born."

Kristi continues to talk, and smile. "Remember to breathe when you're in the bind. Don't tighten. And come out of the bind if you feel any pain. Go to your edge, but no further."

Archina isn't sure where her edge is, but she fears she left it behind several minutes ago. Woo Woo unbinds. She believes in the mind, body, spirit philosophy of yoga, but enough of this shit.

If it's one thing Kristi knows, it's how to read a room full of yogis. The edge has been reached. She tells everyone to stand up, give themselves a hug, and as a special treat, this morning there will be an extended savasana that includes a meditation. (Kristi always has a guided meditation on her phone.) The room smiles, even Bhodi. Eleven bodies move from the vertical to the horizontal.

Archina grabs a blanket; Lexie puts a bolster under her knees; Kevin, the newest member of the group, reaches for his socks.

The Dalai Lama is midway through his 13-minute meditation on the disturbed mind when the studio door opens. Twelve faces turn to look at the human who belongs to the shoes that just clomped into their zen-like state. All twelve agree, zen is overrated. Standing at the entranceway to the studio is a 6'2" man with ripped muscles, ebony skin, and a three-day stubble. "He can bind with me any time he wants," Kevin thinks.

It takes the intruder less than a second to realize he has interrupted the class at an inopportune time. "I'm so sorry," he says. "I thought class was over."

"We're running a little late," says Kristi in a voice the class has not heard before.

"Please continue," says Ripped. "I will come back."

"Too late now," says Bhodi. He gets the evil eye from most of the class.

"How can we help?" says Kristi introducing herself.

Ripped steps forward, hand extended. "My name is Michael ..."

Before he can continue, Woo Woo interjects. "No, it isn't. Your name is Lewis."

The demi-god looks at her in surprise. He's not alone. The whole class stares at Woo Woo.

"I'm so sorry," Woo Woo says turning a deep magenta. "I don't know why I said that." But she does. Sometimes a thought, an image, a tickertape runs through Woo Woo's mind. She knows it's a message, and she usually tries to convey it. On this occasion, she wishes she hadn't.

Michael turns back to Kristi, leader of the pack. "Terrell. Michael Terrell."

"Did you want to join the class?" Bhodi asks. The snark is obvious.

"Please," thinks Kevin. "Please join."

Terrell smiles. "It's on my bucket list, but today I'm here for a less pleasant reason. I'm a detective with the Halifax Police Department. I'm looking into a watch that seems to have gone missing from the gym."

Kristi tries to control her breathing. No one else tries to control anything. Lexie's eyes fly wide open. Charlene gasps. Bonnie recoils.

Honey farts.

It's going to be a big group for coffee today. So much to discuss. Detective Terrell didn't stay long – and he didn't say much. It was what he didn't say that has the group talking in whispers. There's a watch missing (which everyone knew). It's an expensive watch (which everyone surmised). The watch has been stolen (which no one knew, but one person suspected). The police are investigating (hence the ripped detective interrupting savasana). There is much more to this than your run-of-the-mill theft (which almost everyone secretly hopes).

The yoga troupe troops out the studio door. They spot the HPD detective over by the front desk talking to one of the gym's employees. Well, it may be more flirting than talking. Charlene isn't sure what is going on, but she is paying attention. Lexie looks around the gym. So does Kristi, but they're looking for different people. Woo Woo, to everyone's surprise, including her own, walks directly to the front desk and Detective Terrell.

"We always go for coffee after class. Would you like to join us?"

Terrell is taken aback for a moment. But he knows how to hide surprise. He also knows this may be an opportunity to get more information about the theft. Sometimes people don't know what they know. "I'd love to."

Woo Woo leads the way. "My treat," she tells the detective. He orders an Americano. Woo Woo gets him a blueberry muffin as well. "He could stand to put on a few pounds," she thinks.

No one quite knows what to do with a detective at the table. Terrell is used to this discomfort. It's usually a sign of innocence. "Thank you," he says looking around the table. "Most people like to stay as far away from me as possible during an investigation." Everyone laughs. Some even mean it.

"Seems a lot of hoo-ha for a watch," says Lexie looking the detective in the eye.

"We take every theft seriously," says Terrell. It's one of the department's key messages.

Bonnie snorts. Honey shoots her a look. Terrell smiles. "It's also a very nice watch. A Nautilus 7010."

"Jesus," says Charlene almost choking on her cheese Danish. The group turns as one. "That's not a 'nice' watch," she tells them. "That's at least a $60,000 watch."

Terrell is interested to know how the short woman with the purple streak in her grey hair knows this, but in this second he's more interested at the reaction around the room. Most everyone gasps. The round, darkhaired woman stiffens. The yoga instructor pales. And he swears someone farted.

Terrell looks at Charlene. "You're right. This is a very, very nice watch."

"It's much more than that," says Honey. "It's theft over $5,000, and that can land someone in jail for ten years. Grand larceny is a serious offense." Now everyone turns to look at her.

"How do you lose a $60,000 watch?" Archina wonders.

"It's not lost," Terrell reminds her gently.

The reminder seems to hit home. The watch has been stolen. Someone in a place where they find peace, and joy, and friendship has reduced this special connection to a common crime. Several people drop their chins and look down.

Charlene is not one of them. "To rephrase Archina's question, 'How does someone make it easy enough to have their $60,000 watch stolen?"

"What makes you think it was easy?" counters Terrell.

One point for the police officer, Woo Woo thinks. Bhodi grins his approval. Charlene has been an auditor long enough though to meet resistance with aplomb – and grit. "Anyone who buys a Patek Philippe is making a statement. A financial statement. These people watch their money. Closely."

Terrell wants to spend more time in conversation with purple streak, but he also wants to read the table. It's the yoga instructor and the round woman he's most interested in. "Do any of you use the lockers?" Terrell asks putting his media training to good use and shifting direction.

Everyone shakes their head no. To take yoga classes at Asana, you need to be a member of the gym, and that entitles you to a locker. None of the yogis though are interested in lifting weights or tackling a treadmill. It's exercise without the mind, spirit components. Because they don't sweat it out in the fitness room, they don't need to shower or change. They come in their yoga clothes and bring their mats and props with them or use those provided by the studio. It's easier and it keeps them away from the perspiration that pervades the gym.

"Was the watch stolen from his locker?" Bhodi asks with a hint of delight.

"It seems so," says Terrell.

"How would you get into someone's locker?" Kristi asks. "Everyone has their own key or combination."

Terrell nods noncommittally. "That's like saying everyone has their own password," Kevin points out. "And we know how secure that is."

"Glad I don't use the lockers," says Bonnie. Kristi pales even more.

The group slowly starts to dissipate. There is nothing more to be learned here. Terrell takes his time leaving in case anyone has something they want to tell him when he is alone.

Someone does.

Only Woo Woo remains. It's clear she is waiting for the last of her yoga friends to leave. Terrell waits with her making a show of gathering up his cup and plate. "Thank you," Woo Woo says. He didn't make that good a show of it.

"I wanted to apologize for earlier. Sometimes I open my mouth and words come out before my brain has a chance to kick in."

Terrell looks at her closely. She has deep blue eyes set in a face with round cheeks and smile lines. She must be in her early sixties, likely well to do. She has skin that is treated to regular facials. "Not to worry. No harm done," says Terrell.

Then to his own surprise, he adds, "My mother's birth name was Lewis."

"I know," says Woo Woo.

Michael Terrell is off his game. He blames the blue-eyed woman in the tie-dyed yoga outfit. The thing with his mother has him rattled. Terrell's mother died more than 20 years ago when Terrell was in his early thirties. They were close. Truth be told, she was his best friend. Not something a grown man often admits, and certainly not something a seasoned police detective says out loud. Or even to himself.

He's not sure what all that stuff was about knowing his mother was a Lewis. There is no way a stranger could have known that, and no way is Terrell buying into any psychic ability crap. Thirty years with the Halifax Police Department has taught him that out-of-body BS is exactly that. He's not falling for any woo-woo shit. Ahh, now he gets it. Her name.

The detective laughs. Then he shrugs, not tossing off so much an annoyance from the present but an unexpected ache from the past. The gym is busy. There are several people working out on the ellipticals, treadmills, and rowing machines. Several more are lifting weights. None of them look happy.

Terrell heads to the front desk. A young woman, mid-thirties, long blond hair, reed thin, no waist, is behind the counter. She looks up and smiles. Clearly she doesn't know who he is. The detective introduces himself and waits for her muscles to tense, her eyes widen, and her lips narrow. There it is.

Ariel McKinley is a personal trainer. She's been with Vitality+ for more than six years and works the first shift of the day, from 6 a.m. to 2 p.m. Terrell already has this information compliments of Jaxx, but he lets Ariel tell him again. "This is about the watch, isn't it?" Ariel says.

"It is," says Terrell. He stops to look around the gym. "Would you mind if I poke around. I'll need to talk with you later, but for now I'd like to get more comfortable with the layout of the gym."

"Why do you need to talk to me?" Ariel asks. Terrell can feel the tension despite her efforts to appear nonchalant. A typical response.

"We'll need to talk to everyone that was here that morning," the detective says. He turns and heads toward the exercise area.

There really isn't much to see that he didn't expect to see. The gym itself is to the left of the front entranceway and takes up most of the visible floor area. There is a designated cardiovascular zone with the required ellipticals and treadmills. The functional fitness section is packed with battle ropes, medicine balls, kettlebells, power plates, and kinesis stations. There's a free weights space, a stretching and mobility area, and two corners for the personal trainers. Looks much like any gym Terrell has ever been to, and he's been to a lot. This one is newer, and the equipment is fancier. The aroma of stale sweat has not yet permeated the walls, floors, equipment, and staff.

To the right of the front entranceway is the yoga studio. Slightly beyond that are two doors: one changeroom for men and one for women. Terrell makes his way to Byron Newhouse's locker. There is a standard padlock with key slot. Terrell wonders why someone who wears a Patek Philippe watch does not have a more expensive lock that opens via blue tooth or fingerprint. He makes a note to ask.

Now the lock is securely fastened. Terrell gives a hard pull. The two men in the changing room with him turn to look. He smiles and makes his way to the yoga studio.

Kristi is between classes. She takes Terrell on a quick tour. It's like almost every other yoga studio in town – and beyond. Practice area, storage area, entrance way for notices and placement of props for the class. Terrell does not know all this is standard. He doesn't do yoga, although he is a little intrigued. He pokes about the storage area for a minute and finds exactly what he expected: nothing.

He thanks Kristi and makes his way to the door. "Have you found anything?" she asks.

It's a common question, but there is an edge to her voice. Terrell stops and looks at her closely, but gently. "It's a process. We're just getting started."

Participants are starting to file into the studio. Terrell takes a quick look to see if he recognizes anyone. When he is back outside, he makes a note to look a little more closely into the co-owner of the gym.

Daily Thoughts – Shondra (Woo Woo) Aeron Tuesday, October 5th

Keeping a journal, diary, notebook, logbook, whatever you want to call it, is second nature to Woo Woo. She's been doing this since she was a young girl. It's an integral part of her, and she takes the task seriously. So seriously she writes her daily thoughts: pen and paper. It seems to express a greater commitment and a more human connection. Although the laptop would be easier.

I had an insight today. I guess that's what I'm calling them now. This lovely detective came to see us in yoga class, and his mother (I'm sure it was his mother) gave me his name. Well, she gave me her name. And

I corrected him. It was sooooo embarrassing. I apologized. He was very nice about it.

Mind you, the reason he was there in the first place isn't nice. There has been a theft at the gym. Not the yoga studio. We're all okay. (I hope.) Someone took a man's watch worth $60,000. Honey says it's like stealing a Porsche, and the police will devote resources to investigating thoroughly. That's how Honey talks sometimes.

My guess is that we haven't heard the end of this. I mean, the thief has to be a gym member, staff person, or stranger. The latter is unlikely. You need a swipe card to get through the front door, and there is usually someone at the front desk like that nice man Lexie likes. I really thought she was gay. (Is it still "gay" if you're a woman?)

So that leaves someone I've likely seen, maybe even spoken with. Perhaps the detective's mother will help me out. If she knows anything.

Kristi is worried. I mean, who wouldn't be. This is her livelihood, and reputation. I'm not sure, of course, but I'm guessing they still owe a lot for the business. That equipment looks new. And expensive. Not that I would know, mind you. I'm not getting anywhere near it. It all smells of sweat. I wonder if Detective Terrell works out.

Not that it matters. We'll all be here, I'm sure, to support Kristi through whatever comes next. I hope they find out who did it soon. It's a little creepy to think someone is going through your things. I don't envy Detective Terrell his job.

I've found this lovely recipe for vegan blueberry muffins. The afternoon is free – no appointments today. I think I'll make the muffins, and I can take some to class tomorrow morning. In case anyone would like a treat.

Sincerely,
Shondra Aeron

Chapter 5.

Kristi is filling the diffuser when the first participant walks in. Charlene is almost immediately followed by Honey. Kristi would like to think it's excitement about the class; she fears otherwise. Within a few minutes, Lexie and Bhodi arrive. Now Kristi knows something is up.

It's another full class. Kristi wishes dedication to yoga could be as satisfying as the potential for scandal and drama, but she has an ace up her sleeve. Rope pose. Kristi knows how to get even. Gently and respectfully, of course.

Rope pose is a squat and a bind. Even Bhodi struggles. Bonnie and Archina don't make it into the squat. Lexie and Charlene tip over before the bind. Kevin just sits down and wraps his arms around his back. Bhodi and Woo Woo make the squat and the bind but can't sustain the pose. Honey farts.

It's a challenging pose and perfectly in keeping with the theme of the month, but several of the participants suspect they are being punished. Honey and Lexie feel a little chagrined. Woo Woo is embarrassed. Charlene is annoyed. So much for a zen-like state. By savasana though, all is forgiven, on both sides. Everyone, except Bhodi, acknowledges what they could have done better as a yogi and a person.

The to-do around the watch has dissipated. There is no detective, no screaming gym member, no searching high and low. The thought of coffee attracts the core group; the others head off to work, to home, or to run errands. Their loss.

The group is midway through their lattes and Danishes when Michael Terrell shows up. "Mind if I join you?" He pulls out a chair and sits down. From somewhere, a coffee materializes. "I'm just about to head up to the gym." Terrell talks as if this meeting is a regular occurrence. "Thought I'd grab a coffee first. Could be a long day."

He has two people at the table intrigued, one concerned, and one terrified. Terrell continues to chat about the weather and how quickly fall is turning into winter. Finally, Lexie leans forward. "What are you really doing here?"

Terrell feigns surprise, albeit not well. Charlene wonders if this is on purpose. "I'm doing interviews today with staff and members. Thought it would be easier to do them here since the gym is a central location for everyone."

"What are you looking for?" Lexie presses. Kristi thinks the answer to that is obvious. Terrell must too. He doesn't answer the question. "I'm going to be using your office," he says to Kristi, "in case Jaxx didn't tell you." Kristi turns a bright red and blanches at the same time. Woo Woo wonders how she does that.

"Sorry we can't be any help. We were in the middle of yoga class when the watch was stolen." Charlene states the obvious but wants that fact out there. What the hell, she wonders, is going on with Kristi?

"Do you have any suspects?" asks Lexie trying to sound nonchalant. She fails.

"I do," says Terrell. Everyone leans forward. The detective leans back and slowly sips his coffee. "I guess it's time for me to head to the office."

As he makes his way out the door, Woo Woo runs after him. She has a bag of blueberry muffins in her hand and thrusts them toward the detective. "I brought these in as a treat today. Thought you might like some."

Terrell smiles. Woo Woo beams. "Thank you. I'll enjoy these."

He's lying. Terrell doesn't like blueberries, and he suspects they're vegan.

The Interviews: Part 1
Wednesday, October 6ᵗʰ

Byron Newhouse

Terrell's first interview is with Byron Newhouse. This is deliberate. He's already got the details of the theft from Byron, but he'd like to dig a little deeper. The theft could be for financial gain, or it could be personal. To determine if it's the latter, Terrell needs to know the watch owner a little better.

Newhouse makes it quite clear in the first few seconds of the interview that he is a busy man, and he really doesn't have time for this. In the next breath, he demands a progress update, making it obvious he thinks the master criminal should have been caught by now.

All this rolls off Michael Terrell's back like water off a duck. Not the first person he's interviewed with money, ego, and entitlement. "Could you tell me why you had your watch with you. It's an expensive watch." Terrell ignores Newhouse's bleating and moves him in the direction he wants him to go.

"Of course, it's an expensive watch," hisses Newhouse like Terrell is an idiot. Doesn't bother Terrell (the water thing). In fact, this is what the detective wants: to see how Newhouse reacts. So far, not a likeable man.

"I work out with my son. Well, now my son and his girlfriend." Newhouse says this like someone has poured vinegar in his mouth. "From here, I go to work. I change into my work clothes here. That includes my watch."

"Still," Terrell pushes, "rather an expensive watch to wear to work every day."

Newhouse smiles. It's closer to a sneer, actually. And he ignores the question. "What do you really want to know?"

Terrell gives Newhouse points for being brighter than expected. He leans in. "Your watch is worth a lot of money. Someone might want cash. Or someone might just want to stick it to you. Any ideas who?"

Unexpectedly Newhouse sits back. Terrell can see the look on his face. It's not surprise. It's fear. Something hit home. Newhouse tries to correct, but it's too late. He recognizes that. The next step in situations like this, at least in Terrell's experience, is to point the finger of blame in another direction far away from the person you really believe committed the crime.

As if on cue, Newhouse bends forward, a conspiratorial air. "I didn't want to say this, but I'm worried my son's girlfriend, Jade, might have taken the watch. I don't trust her, and she needs money."

And there it is. The real suspect. Byron Newhouse thinks his son is a thief.

Christian Newhouse

Christian Newhouse is the opposite of his father. The father is beefy; the son is slender. The father is all bluster and bravado, the son is reticent and still. Terrell wonders if this is Christian's natural state of being or if an interview with the police has the young man turning inward. It's a survival mechanism Terrell has seen many times before.

The detective has two choices. He can come at Byron Newhouse's son hard and push the information he wants out of the young man, or he can play nice and nudge it out gently. If there is anything to nudge.

It's almost time for a break, and Terrell is thinking he'll try one of the blueberry muffins. In that spirit of openness, he opts for door number two. But he will come down hard on the kid if he has to.

The kid is actually 28, but he seems younger. That may be the reticence. It could also be guilt. His father certainly thinks so. Terrell dives in. "Your father is pretty upset about his watch."

"Yes." Christian looks at the floor.

Terrell nudges. "What do you think happened?"

"His watch was stolen."

The HPD detective doesn't know what the hell is going on, but he has now committed to the blueberry muffin, and he doesn't have the time or the patience for stating the obvious. "Kid, we can do this one of two ways. We can have an adult discussion, or I can take the lead. If I do that, let me assure you, it will be uncomfortable."

Christian slumps. "I don't know what you want from me."

"It's simple. I want your insight into what you think happened to your father's watch."

Christian opens his mouth. "Don't tell me it was stolen," says Terrell. Christian closes his mouth.

Terrell makes an abrupt shift. "Your father doesn't like your girlfriend."

"No," says Christian. "I mean, yes."

"Glad we could clear that up." Terrell smiles. So does the kid.

"Everybody likes Jade. Everybody but my dad. She's smart – she's getting her PhD in environmental law; she's caring – she volunteers at an animal shelter and sits with seniors. And she never says a bad word about anybody."

"She sounds wonderful."

Christian nods. Terrell can see him start to relax. "So why doesn't your dad like her?"

"She doesn't have money." Christian says this simply as if talking about the weather forecast. "She lives in a basement apartment near the university, and she buys her clothes at Value Village."

"That must rankle." Christian looks up quizzically. "Great girlfriend, petty-minded father."

The detective expected the son to come to the defense of his father, offer up some small justification or attempt to put the bigotry in context.

Instead, Christian nods his agreement.

* * *

Terrell is rereading his notes. There isn't much else to do, and this might help him get ready for his next interview with Jade Dhillon. Byron Newhouse is 51. He's CEO of Bluenose Developments and worth many millions. At least the company is. Terrell writes down: check Newhouse's finances. He sits on several boards, including Saint Mary's University and the Chamber of Commerce. He has been married to Sylvia for 27 years. He is a bully.

Christian Newhouse is 28, a PhD candidate in management (if you can believe it) at Dalhousie University. Terrell wonders if Christian, an only child, is being primed to take over the father's construction business. He makes a note.

It's what's not in the notes that Terrell focuses on while he sips a dark roast and eats the first of two blueberry muffins. (They're really not bad.) The watch is definitely gone. It could be an insurance scam, which would make daddy guilty. But Terrell saw fear on Byron Newhouse's face when he asked about suspects. Terrell knows fear. He sees it every day.

So, if the watch was really stolen, the son is a prime suspect. He knows about the watch, he knows its value, and he knows his dad leaves it in the locker when he works out. He might even know how to get his hands on the key or make a duplicate. But why? The kid doesn't like to tangle with his father, and he doesn't need money.

But his girlfriend does.

Terrell makes a note to find out just how badly Jade Dhillon needs cash.

Jade Dhillon

There is one other thing Christian failed to mention about his girlfriend: she's East Indian. Terrell isn't sure if this is the correct term, but Jade Dhillon's ancestry can undoubtedly be traced back to India. She has lovely brown skin and thick black hair. Terrell can admire both. Indeed, he has both in his own right albeit of a different ancestry. What's most relevant now about Jade's heritage is how Byron Newhouse might feel about his son dating a woman of color. Terrell doesn't think it would go over well, but that might be his bias about the father coming through.

Jade Dhillon is composed, articulate, and polite. She's also all business. "What do you want to know?"

"Did you steal Byron Newhouse's watch?"

"No." Jade doesn't flinch. Her eyes never leave Terrell's face.

"What do you think happened?"

"I think Byron Newhouse got exactly what he deserved." Jade's eyes remain firmly on Terrell's face.

The detective wavers. This he did not see coming. Jade continues either unaware the impact her statement has made or indifferent to it. "Byron is a showoff. He flashes that watch around for everyone to see, and if he thinks you don't know its value, he manages to work that into the conversation, no matter how brief.

"Byron is also an idiot." Jade continues without pausing. "He misplaces his locker key, as well as his car key, his phone, and his ear buds, at least once a day. In fact, he misplaces his changeroom key so often, he keeps a spare in his car, which is often left unlocked 'cause he can't find the key to lock it."

Jade takes a second to breathe. Terrell takes advantage of the opening. "Still, if someone found a locker key, they would have to know it was Byron's and that it opened the door to an expensive watch."

"What if they didn't find it?" Jade counters. Terrell waits. "What if someone in the gym took the key when Byron wasn't looking."

"He usually keeps the key in his sweats. You'd have to be pretty clever to get your hand in a man's pants without alerting said man."

Jade counterthrusts. "And he throws his pants over the bench while he showers."

This is all very helpful. Too helpful, Terrell thinks. Jade has made an excellent case for a stranger stealing Byron Newhouse's expensive Nautilus watch.

She thinks her boyfriend took it.

* * *

It's lunch. Terrell heads to the coffee shop. On the way out, he walks over to the yoga studio. If Woo Woo is taking another class, he'll thank her for the delicious muffins. Surprisingly, at least to Kristi and the rest of the class, Woo Woo is doing her second practice of the day. She spies Terrell on her way out. He smiles. She turns pink. He thanks her for the muffins. She turns pinker. Terrell suggests they grab a bite. Woo Woo is afraid she might spontaneously combust.

Lunch runs a little longer than Terrell had anticipated, and he arrives back at the gym just in time for his next round of interviews. Turns out there is no next round of interviews. Jaxx has been unexpectedly called out to a meeting, and the two personal trainers are heading home for the day after their shift. They ask for a reprieve. Terrell reschedules for the next day making it clear if they don't show up, the interviews will be held at the police station. It's a message they are also to deliver to Jaxx.

Daily Thoughts – Kristi Yee
Wednesday, October 6th

As the yoga instructor, Kristi doesn't feel obligated to do the monthly activity every day, or at all, truth be told. But she knows there is a release in getting things off your chest, in sharing what is inside with the outside world. Kristi should be reaching for pen and paper; instead, she turns on her laptop and opens a new blank document.

She stares at the screen. She saves the file: daily thoughts.oct6. She hovers her fingers above the keyboard. Kristi is not a trained typist, but this shouldn't take long. She cleans her keyboard. She stretches. She hovers again.

Finally, Kristi types.

Something is terribly wrong.

The Interviews: Part 2
Thursday, October 7th

Jaxx Taylor

The co-owner of Vitality+ is tall, at least 6' with thick black hair and a muscular frame. He is a good-looking man, Terrell thinks. He thinks this dispassionately. It is his job to observe. Observations can lead to assumptions, at the very least questions, that, in turn, can lead to evidence.

Jaxx is impatient. At least that is the pretense he is putting forward. A man used to getting what he wants without having to work very hard for it. He gets by on looks, maybe even personality. Terrell writes in his notebook. Jaxx looks up, trying to look indifferent, but Terrell knows what indifference really looks like.

"Sorry we couldn't do this yesterday. I got called out at the last minute."

Terrell nods. "I know you've done this a dozen times already, but could you run me through the morning Byron Newhouse's watch went missing."

The gym owner sighs. Audibly. Clearly this is an inconvenience. Terrell writes in his notebook.

"I opened the gym at 5:45. Newhouse, his son, and the girlfriend arrived around 7:00. They exercised for about 45 minutes. Nathan was working with Byron. At about ten to eight, Byron comes out of the changeroom screaming about his watch."

"And you saw all this?"

"Most of it. I mean I didn't stare at them the whole time they were here, but I waved when they arrived and saw them on the floor. I was in the office when Byron came out frothing at the mouth, but I moved to the front desk pretty quickly."

"Could anybody walk into the gym and steal the watch from his locker?"

"Nope." Jaxx sounds sure of this. "You can't get into the changerooms without a keycard. It's even hard to get past the front desk without one of us seeing."

"So how could a watch go missing?"

Jaxx tries to hide his eye roll, but not that hard. "You don't think the watch went missing," Terrell says, then he waits. Jaxx is champing at the bit to share his theory.

The gym owner leans in. "This is an insurance scam. Newhouse needs money."

Now, this is new. The information and the animosity. "What makes you think that?"

"There's no way anyone would know what locker matches a lost key, and they wouldn't have time to randomly try lockers if that's what you're thinking. There is always someone coming and going into the changerooms.

"And Newhouse isn't as liquid as he pretends," Jaxx adds. "I just wish he'd pay his damn gym bill."

Terrell writes some more in his notebook. It's a stall tactic. Certainly, insurance fraud is always a prime consideration when anything valuable goes missing. To date, Newhouse hasn't filed a claim. The implication is he's hoping to get his watch back.

Jaxx is bored with the stall tactic. He rises from his chair and heads for the door. As he's about to exit, he turns and looks Terrell in the eye. "If it wasn't the father, it was his kid who stole the watch."

Ariel McKinley

The physical trainer moves into Jaxx's spot almost as soon as he leaves the room. Ariel McKinley, tall and slim, has her long blonde hair tied back in a ponytail. She may have had a boob job. Terrell thinks she didn't need one.

"I'm not sure I'm going to be much help." Ariel's voice is calm, her statement direct. It's a sentiment Terrell hears often, although usually with less assurance.

"Can you tell me where you were the morning the theft happened and what you saw."

"I saw the triumvirate arrive, waved hello, and went about my tasks. Next thing Newhouse is screaming bloody murder."

"What are your tasks, other than being a physical trainer for clients?"

"All of us, even Jaxx and Kristi, work to make sure the gym is clean and uncluttered. We pick up dirty towels and water cups that people leave everywhere. We run a load of laundry through. We work the front desk, answering questions and welcoming clients."

"Sounds a little mundane." Terrell is hoping to get a rise. He's not sure if he does.

"Look, this is a successful gym. There are clients coming out the yin yang. One reason for this: they know the staff. We stick around because Jaxx and Kristi pay us well to stick around. If that means running a load of laundry, so be it." There is a hint of defiance in Ariel's voice, but it is so subtle Terrell thinks he may have misread it.

"How many clients would you have?"

"Why does it matter?" Ariel shifts forward in her chair, a move Terrell is familiar with, but he's not through with her yet. He waits.

"Nathan and I usually have about 20 clients each, but this varies from week to week, and clients don't always book a trainer. Sometimes they just work out."

"But Newhouse had a trainer."

"He likes to show us how much better he is than everyone else. Likes to flaunt his superiority even to a lowly fitness trainer. It's like that watch. It says to the world how special he isn't."

"You don't like him."

"I don't like his type," says Ariel. "I don't give a shit about him."

Terrell writes in his notebook: Methinks the lady doth protest too much.

Nathan Young

Nathan Young doesn't look like a personal trainer. That's Terrell's first thought. The man's upper arms don't strain his t-shirt and his legs don't resemble tree trunks. Indeed, Nathan almost appears average: height, weight, hair color. Look closely though and muscles are well defined, posture is straight, core is strong, and there is an ease of movement that only the naturally athletic have.

There is also a nervous air about Nathan, but Terrell feels this is more about deference or self-doubt than worry about the interview. He takes a few minutes to discuss Nathan's job with him and put him at ease. The trainer clearly likes his job.

"How is Byron Newhouse as a client?"

"He's committed." Nathan is giving nothing away. "A lot of our regulars have that dedication."

"Why would dedicated members need a trainer?" Terrell asks this without rancor.

"Everyone can benefit from a trainer." Nathan sits a little straighter. Terrell thinks it's starting to sound like a brochure. Time to move on. "Tell me about that morning."

"Not much to tell. Byron, Christian, and Jade arrived shortly after we opened and came out of the changerooms after a few minutes. I was waiting on the floor for Byron, and we worked for about 45 minutes as scheduled."

"Is that your normal routine?"

Nathan hesitates. "I haven't been training Byron that long, but he likes to come in first thing and get out so he can start work as early as possible."

"Why did you start training Byron?"

A little more hesitation. Terrell isn't sure if it's contemplation or consternation. "Ariel used to work with Byron, but it's good for clients to work with different trainers. We like to mix it up."

"What's Byron like to work with?" Terrell asks again. "I mean as a person."

"He's a busy man and has a lot on his mind. He can be a little abrupt at times, but it's not personal."

"Ariel thinks he's arrogant and offensive."

"He's not the nicest man at times," Nathan agrees, "but I'm not sure what that has to do with his watch being stolen."

"Maybe nothing, maybe everything. Sometimes people steal things not for money but for personal reasons. They want to get even, they want to hurt someone, they want to cause distress."

Clearly that has never occurred to Nathan. Terrell writes in his notebook: nice guy. "Tell me something. Just between you and me. If you had to name the thief, what name would you give me."

Nathan is clearly uncomfortable, but Terrell feels that is more about the man being nice than any inside knowledge. Finally, Nathan looks up. He says softly, "Christian."

Flavor of the month. "Why?" Terrell asks.

The answer surprises him. "Christian loves Jade. Jade needs money."

Terrell reviews his notes and takes his time putting things in his briefcase. He checks his watch (a black stainless steel Fossil, retail $170). He tells himself he's surprised it's lunchtime and slowly exits the office. The yoga class is exiting next door. Terrell smiles. It doesn't last. Small class and no one he recognizes.

Chapter 6.

Nathan thinks that went well, although he is not sure how one defines "well" in these situations. He feels good about his answers; they were honest, and he didn't besmirch anyone's reputation. Admittedly, he did finger Christian as the culprit (as James Patterson would say), but that was not done nastily. And the reason is so relatable: love.

The fitness trainer smiles at himself. He does love love. Even though, at the moment, he doesn't have a love interest of his own. He is a little concerned about that yoga woman. She seems to have taken a fancy to him. Good grief, she's old enough to be his mother. Not that age matters.

What Nathan is most relieved about, he admits to himself, is not having to talk more about Byron Newhouse. He's not a nice man, but Nathan would rather not have to say that out loud. Nathan understands why Ariel dropped him as a client, although he would have liked a little more advance notice. Still, it all worked out in the end, Nathan thinks.

It's not his nature to look at how situations benefit him; however, because Ariel dropped Newhouse, Nathan was his trainer when the watch went missing.

Almost impossible for anyone to think Nathan was the thief. I mean Newhouse had the watch when he arrived. Nathan was on the floor waiting for him and still there when the watch was discovered missing.

"I hope Christian didn't do it," Nathan says to himself. "He wouldn't do well in jail." Then again, who does? And what is the likelihood Byron Newhouse would let his only kid go to jail over a watch. Undeniably an expensive watch. What idiot wears that kind of jewelry to a gym?. Even if it doesn't go missing, it could get broken while you're changing or wet from towels and freshly showered arms.

That's what Ariel and Jaxx said, too. Of course, we're all defensive about the reputation of Vitality+, Nathan acknowledges to himself. If word gets out that stuff gets stolen here, that will not be good for business, and Nathan likes his job. He also needs this job. He has been with Jaxx (and Kristi) since they opened seven years ago, and that gives him seniority and a great deal of freedom. It lets him do what he loves most: surfing. Nathan already has plans to go to Hawaii next summer, maybe earlier.

He grabs a load of towels and heads for the men's changeroom still pondering the interview. He's not sure now that he helped Detective Terrell. He's a little disappointed in himself. He opens the door to the changeroom and nods at two regulars. He makes his way to the showers and the towel racks. They're fully stocked. Ariel made it there before him. "That was nice of her," he thinks.

He heads back out to the floor. The detective is just leaving. Nathan waves and walks toward him. "I'm not sure I was much help. Sorry."

"You were very helpful." Terrell is being polite. He doesn't really mean it. Turns out, he should have.

Chapter 7.

Kristi has reached a decision. It wasn't an easy decision, and she is still not convinced it is the right decision. But it has been made. She will see it through.

For most of her life, Kristi has been doing yoga. It's as natural to her as breathing. For most of her adult life, Kristi has been teaching yoga. In all that time, she can count on one hand the students who have become friends, and all of those people have gone on to become yoga instructors themselves. While Kristi is friendly with her students and will go out of her way to support them on their yoga journey, becoming friends is a line she is reluctant to cross. Today she fears she will.

The yoga studio is full. This doesn't bode well for Kristi and her line in the sand. She leads the group through a series of poses, several quite difficult. She starts with bound extended side angle and looks to see who goes down. Archina and Kevin stumble. She ramps it up a little with a bound forward fold and hears several groans. Kristi smiles to herself. She throws out a challenge: bound warrior three. Bhodi is up for it, which means Charlene will also go to her edge. Several people teeter, and only Bhodi can clasp his hands behind his back. A series of vinyasa flows follow. Kristi warns them with each flow, she's going to pump up the pace. She does. The group collapses into savasana.

Kristi makes it fairly quick. She wants them to unwind and rebound, but she still wants them feeling an ache or twinge that will get them heading for home or the office, not coffee. When Honey asks who is going for coffee, only three hands cut through the air. Things are going well, Kristi thinks. Maybe it's a sign she has made the right decision.

Lexie, Charlene, Woo Woo, and Honey head for the café. Kristi joins them once she has tidied the studio. The women have a soy latte waiting for her and a chocolate chip cookie. They're in the middle of a debate over whether paper coffee cups can be composted. Haligonians take their composting seriously. Honey votes with her feet. She checks her phone, says she has to run, and tosses her disposable cup in the garbage on her way out. Charlene laughs. Woo Woo gasps.

The others are starting the winding-up ritual: napkins are crumpled on top of plates, purses are plopped on the table, chairs start to scrape back. Kristi coughs. She feels their glances. "Would you mind staying a few more minutes?"

Instantly, the chairs return to their original positions. "Of course," says Lexie speaking for the group.

There is a moment of awkwardness. No one wants to be seen to presume a problem. Everyone assumes there is. "I need your help." Kristi sounds close to tears. Woo Woo pats her hand.

Kristi dives in. "I think there is something funny going on with the gym's finances, and I need you to help me find out what."

All three women lean in. They're trying to look sympathetic; they're feeling thrilled. Charlene takes the lead. Finances are her thing. "What do you think is going on?"

"I don't know," Kristi admits. "Jaxx has been avoiding my questions about money for months now. He assures me the business is doing well, but he doesn't hand over the files even though I have repeatedly asked for them."

"Don't you have access to the bank statements?" Charlene asks.

"Sort of. We're a partnership on paper and, I thought, philosophically, but in reality, Jaxx has looked after the gym and the financial side of the business. We're supposed to meet monthly to keep each other apprised. That hasn't been happening, and Jaxx has put a password on his computer, so I can't get into the files without him."

The three women at the table look grim, especially Charlene. Woo Woo gets more coffee. Decaf. "How can we help?" Lexie asks.

"I'm going to get the files off his computer, but I can't do it alone."

"Count me in," says Lexie. The other two nod.

"Once we have the files," Kristi says looking at Charlene, "I was hoping you could go through them and tell me what's what."

"Glad to," says Charlene. "So how do we get them."

Jaxx is sitting in his office staring at his computer, but really not looking at what's on the screen. His mind is elsewhere. He thinks he handled the cop well, but still the damn watch is a pain in his side. Byron is still blathering on about it, although not quite as loudly. Jaxx hopes they arrest Christian soon, and the whole thing will end. On the plus side, Kristi seems to have backed off asking about the books, as he knew she would. He knows how to handle her.

A knock at his open office door brings him back to this earthly plane. There's a woman standing there Jaxx feels he should know. Her face is familiar. She appears to be wearing a caftan.

"Do you have a minute?" Woo Woo asks.

"Of course." Jaxx welcomes her into the office.

"I was hoping for a tour." Woo Woo stays put at the entranceway.

Jaxx gets up. He hopes she can't hear him sigh.

"I'm Shondra, but everybody calls me Woo Woo." As they begin the tour, Woo Woo tells him she is a member of the gym but has only used the yoga studio. She thinks she might like to exercise. Jaxx knows now why she looks so familiar.

The tour takes much longer than it usually does. I mean, there really isn't much to see in a gym. Gym equipment, changing rooms, introductions to the staff. But this woman is a talker, and she has lots of questions. He's not sure some of them make sense.

After 20 minutes, she has run out of questions. Jaxx invites her to try the gym out for a few days and offers up a personal trainer, complimentary, for her first two visits. Woo Woo seems delighted.

"I do have one last question." Jaxx can't wait. "It's a little silly, but I wondered what you think of my outfit."

If Jaxx didn't know any better, he'd think this woman was stalling. He knows better: she is a bit of a wing nut. He tells her the caftan is lovely. She tells him it's a yukata and thanks him for the tour. Jaxx heads back to the office. As he passes the front desk, he sees another woman he swears is also in the yoga group talking to Nathan. Maybe a gym/studio crossover is possible.

He reaches his office door and turns the knob. "Funny. I didn't think I shut the door."

By the time Woo Woo gets down to the café, the other three have secured a table; croissants and an assortment of herbal teas are waiting. They let Woo Woo make the first selection. She picks a pomegranate and chamomile blend and a chocolate croissant. She feels like celebrating. The others agree. There are grins all round.

"I hate to admit this," says Lexie, "but that was fun. Almost exciting."

"I was scared to death," says Kristi. "Certain we'd get caught downloading those files."

Charlene tilts her head to one side. "I was okay once we accessed the files. I was worried the encrypted screensaver would kick in before we reached the desk."

"I could feel Jaxx getting twitchy by the end," says Woo Woo. "I don't know if I could have kept him away from the office for much longer."

"I could have stepped in," says Lexie, "as planned."

"Your job was to text Kristi and Charlene in the office," Woo Woo reminds her.

"And to support you," says Lexie. "I'm ambidextrous."

Everyone laughs. Kristi reaches into her sweater pocket and pulls out a thumb drive. She puts it on the table. The four women stare at it. "Here is what we risked Jaxx's wrath and potential embarrassment for.

"I'm glad you were with me," she adds, turning to Charlene. "There were so many files."

"We got the bank statements, which is the most important," says Charlene. "That will tell us almost anything we want to know."

Kristi turns a paler shade of white. "Part of me hopes you won't find anything. Part of me knows you will."

Charlene reassures her that, even if she finds "something," it may not be serious or it might be easily fixed. "Let's meet back here tomorrow after yoga. I should know by then most of what we need to know."

Daily Thoughts – Charlene
Thursday, October 7th

What a day! I felt like James Bond meets Catwoman. Those references probably date me. But you know what, I am dated. I'll officially be a senior citizen in four years, but today I was a master criminal. Moved like a stealth bomber with the intellect of Einstein.

Okay, I'm getting carried away. But I had such a good time. Lexie even said that it was fun. I don't think Lexie has a lot of fun. Odd for a comedian when you think of it.

Now, I'll have to get to work and go through the financials. I doubt it will take long to unearth anything, if there is anything there to unearth. Jaxx does not strike me as a financial whiz. I'm more concerned about what I will find and what it will mean for Kristi. It certainly sounds like her partner is hiding something. Not the first time I've seen this. I'm no longer surprised when smart people do stupid things like put responsibility for finances in one person's hands. I had a client once – multimillion dollar company with more than 125 employees – who did not have the password to her own bank accounts. Sadly, it is often a "she" who gets taken.

Not this time if I can help it. I'm going to have a light lunch – maybe a little mac and cheese from the Italian Market with some prosciutto – and I'll hunker down with the books. Who knows, by supper I may have the answers Kristi is looking for.

We're going to meet tomorrow to review everything. Perhaps I'll do up a little PowerPoint this evening. It will be hard to review the PPTX in the café. Not a lot of privacy, and Woo Woo can be loud. Ooh, maybe the women would like to come here. I think I'll suggest that. I'll pick up some frangipane tarts and panna cotta from the market for a treat, and some chicken parmigiana for Madoff. Guess I'd also better do a quick vacuuming.

Sincerely,

Charlene Kurtz

PS Today is my parents' anniversary. I wonder if he knows that.

Chapter 8.

Charlene texts everyone right away. That way she can honestly say she doesn't know what is in the financials but thought they could talk more openly at her place. She includes the address of her condo in Bedford South and mentions the frangipane tarts and panna cotta. It's starting to sound like a social gathering, but everyone will know it's not. Charlene realizes, a little surprised, that this will be the first time any of the yoga group (to her knowledge) have met outside the studio or the café. She thinks that is a good thing. Tomorrow will tell.

Woo Woo is thrilled with the invitation and answers right away. She offers to bring her homemade chai tea (the secret ingredient is star anise). It's a soothing drink. Woo Woo is a little worried they may all need some soothing, especially Kristi. Lexie is also in, but she's not sure what to bring. Sounds like she shouldn't show up empty handed though. Finally, she settles on gluten-free brownies. This seems de rigueur. Lexie hits the "send" button.

It takes several hours for Kristi to respond. She's not avoiding the text. She's teaching classes and staying out of Jaxx's way, which means staying out of the office where she left her phone early this morning. At 6 p.m. her text – saying yes and thank you – arrives. By then, Charlene knows the get together isn't going to be a happy one. Even with the panna cotta and the PowerPoint.

Yoga class was good, as usual, but Charlene's heart wasn't in it. She was more focused on what she needed to do once she got home and before everyone arrived. She was also thinking about how Kristi would react to the information she had to share. Kristi moved them into a bound triangle as the pose of the day. Charlene wasn't overly fond of triangle as a pose and even less so when it was trussed up in a bind. She glanced at Lexie and saw her grimace. Woo Woo seemed to be enjoying herself. Charlene wonders if she uses cannabis.

As soon as class ended, Charlene was out the door. Lexie and Woo Woo said they'd wait for Kristi and everyone would come together in one car. Charlene figured that would give her at least half an hour. In that time, she put the Italian pastries on a tray, carefully placing napkins and good-quality paper plates beside them. She had a pot of coffee on and hot water boiled for tea. Madoff even donned a bow tie. (This required four treats to complete.)

The only outstanding item was where to meet: living room or dining room. The former was nicer and a little more comfortable; the latter was more functional and perhaps friendlier because it seems more casual. People gather around the table to chat. Charlene opted for the dining room. By the time the three women arrived Charlene and Madoff were ready. Charlene welcomed everyone, and they took a few seconds to admire her condo and say what a lovely home she had. Charlene expected this, but it didn't make it any less true. Woo Woo and Kristi spent some time cooing over Madoff, and he forgave Charlene for the bow tie. He did wonder why there were no more treats.

Everyone took a seat at the dining room table. Charlene had a small stack of file folders near the chair at the head of the table, and everyone avoided this spot, including Madoff. (He was hoping some of the guests would drop crumbs; Charlene never did this.)

Charlene suggested they dive in. She looked at Kristi, who was sitting on her left. Kristi nodded. Charlene had confirmed with Kristi that she wanted Lexie and Woo Woo at the meeting. Her affirmation was a little surprising, but Charlene had learned over the course of more than 30 years that the need for a comforting touch or a kind word from a friend often outweighed privacy and confidentiality. In fact, it usually did.

"It's not good," Charlene says. She can hear Kristi suck in her breath. Woo Woo and

Lexie look down at the very nice paper plates. "But it's also not bad." Kristi exhales.

Charlene distributes the file folders with the printed PPTX presentation inside. (She felt this would be easier than trying to set up the projector and that would have required meeting in the living room.) She starts with the revenue slide.

"The business is doing well. As you can see, almost half a million dollars is coming through the door every year and has been for the last several years.

"This figure could be higher," Charlene adds, "with a few efficiency measures and better bill collecting, but Vitality+ is on a solid financial footing when it comes to bringing money in the door."

The three women look up from their printouts. They know what is coming, and expectation hangs heavy in the room. "It's money going out the door that is the problem," Charlene says. Lexie thinks the auditor has milked this moment for dramatic effect. And why not. As Lexie knows, it's not the joke that gets you laughs, it's the delivery.

Woo Woo reaches for Kristi's hand and pats it. Kristi smiles at her, already thankful she asked Woo Woo and Lexie to be here. Kristi takes a deep breath in. "Spell it out for us."

Charlene spends the next 30 minutes doing just that. She points out that expenses have risen by double digits in each of the last five years, and most of those expenses are unnecessary and certainly not offset by incoming revenue. She points to the purchase of six 3G Cardio Elite Runner treadmills as an example of overspending and unnecessary spending. Each machine costs roughly $5,000. This is clearly a quality product, but there are less expensive yet still very good options available. As well, are six machines really necessary especially given the high number of members who use private trainers? If there were only three treadmills and they were all in use, the trainers could give clients other exercises to do.

It's not just treadmills. Jaxx has upgraded equipment twice in the last six years, which may make members happy but does not make for good business. There are also questionable expenses, Charlene points out. There was $10,000 allocated for artwork in 2021, but Charlene doubts there is even $2,000 worth of art in the gym. Posters are not art. She also notes that hospitality and marketing expenses are very high – over $50,000 – but there is no ad budget, print expenses, or social media outlay. She fears Jaxx is having himself a good time at the expense of the company. Literally.

Charlene believes the gym's problems come down to inexperience, arrogance, and an unwillingness to ask for help. (The last reason may simply be another way of saying inexperience and arrogance.) Charlene doesn't hold back. She's learned as an auditor bluntness is your friend. It pushes people to accept the reality of the situation and move to solutions.

Bottom line: Vitality+ owes suppliers, contractors, its landlord, and others more than $350,000.

Kristi is in tears now. They fall softly and quietly on her file folder, her yoga pants, and her frangipani. A noisy crier, Lexie marvels at this ladylike grace. There is no snotting or bawling. Woo Woo hands Kristi a tissue. Lexie wonders why.

Charlene sits back. She doesn't say a word. She waits.

"What does this all mean?" Kristi asks. "Bottom line."

"You have revenue coming in so you have the ability to get your financial footing on solid ground, but it will take at least three years, perhaps longer depending on how willing you are to cut and cut back."

"What do you mean?" Kristi asks.

"Well, I'd start by cutting your salary and Jaxx's by at least a third, a half if you can afford it. I'd let the trainers go and replace them with experienced trainers willing to accept a lower salary. At present, you are paying top dollar."

"That's a little extreme," Lexie says loudly. Everyone looks at her. She recognizes she may have spoken out of turn. "I mean, you want to keep existing members happy.

They may look elsewhere if their trainer leaves."

Charlene nods. "Each decision will have to be weighed. What happens if we do this, what can happen if we don't.

"The number one thing you need to do," she says leaning in. Lexie is impressed with the performance. "Get an independent outside third party to do your books. Right away. That person will set the rules, hold regular meetings, and provide both parties with an accounting of where things stand."

"Will you do it?" Kristi asks. There is a hint of desperation.

Charlene expected this question. Until now, though, she didn't know what her answer would be. She turns and looks at Kristi. "Of course, I will."

The women spend the next hour coming up with ideas as to how the company could spend less and earn more. Some of the ideas are obvious (return any equipment that has not passed its return-by date), others are less obvious but have potential (offer new services like reflexology and pilates), others are a little out there, but what the hell (get rid of the cleaning crew and make Jaxx clean the gym at the end of the day). The last one was Kristi's suggestion.

What to do about Jaxx remains the big issue. The question hovers over the panna cotta and the organic green matcha tea. It infuses the unspoken conversation. It is the elephant in the room.

It must be Kristi who raises the topic, and finally it is. "I'll have to tell Jaxx all this." Everyone nods.

"Do you want us there with you?" Woo Woo asks. She reaches for Kristi's hand and pats it. Lexie thinks the skin might be getting a little raw by now.

Kristi thinks about the offer. There is safety in numbers, and Jaxx can be nasty when cornered. Before she can answer, Charlene says, "You have to tell Jaxx, but you don't have to tell him in person." Kristi, Lexie, Woo Woo, and Madoff turn to look at her.

"Send him an email," Charlene says. "It gives him time to understand what you've discovered, that there is no avoiding the issue, and ideally, time to calm down."

Kristi likes this option. So do Lexie, Woo Woo, and Madoff. The women spend the next 45 minutes drafting the email. Madoff eats the crumbs off the floor.

Daily Thoughts – Lexie
Friday, October 8th

There was nothing fun – or funny – about today. Times like this make me miss stand-up. You know the beige hotel rooms, the gourmet burger served cold, the little mouse in the corner of the dressing room who is your best friend. God, those were the days.

Today was depressing. Maybe not depressing. More like soul suffocating. Kristi's business is in trouble, Kristi's partner has been keeping her in the dark, and there is no way out but through. Through means through numb nuts. We drafted an email, Charlene's idea, to Jaxx so he'd know the jig is up. (Really, "the jig is up?" My podcast better be better than this.) Charlene says if he's going to be really nasty about the situation, he'll respond right away. If he's giving up, he'll take at least two days to respond.

Woo Woo asked what it meant if he took a day to respond. Charlene scooped us all up at that point and we drove over to the Royal Bank. She had Kristi freeze the company's account, which means that no money can come out of the account, but money can go in. This will be a little tricky for suppliers like the power company that have automatic withdrawals, but we all agreed we would contact these companies and give them a credit card number to bill. That was the second thing Kristi did; she deactivated the company's current credit card and opened a new one.

We went back to Charlene's to tie up loose ends and eat lunch, smoked turkey with Swiss cheese on focaccia. I had two, well, one and a half. I shared with Madoff. Charlene had a form she uses for the credit bureaus. It prevents anyone (i.e., Jaxx) from opening any new accounts in the company's name, including credit cards. So, he should be out of options to take any more money from the company.

Kristi was obviously relieved and, at the same time, worried sick. She will have to face Jaxx. Woo Woo and I offered to be there for moral support; Charlene is going to be there for her business expertise and as the company's new accountant. I pity the old one.

Then Kristi hit "send" on the email to Jaxx. It will rock his world. She started by saying she had frozen the bank account and cancelled the credit card. That ought to get his attention. Then just when we thought we could relax, I decided to open my big mouth. Not sure if I was the only one thinking this, but you have a man with financial troubles and a very expensive stolen watch. One plus one in my mind.

Kristi was obviously horrified. Apparently, the thought hadn't occurred to her, or she pushed it into the recesses of her mind. Charlene agreed it was a real possibility; Woo Woo tried to reassure Kristi "surely not" until I pointed out we would have to tell the cop. At which point, Woo Woo reconsidered her position. Straight women are so predictable.

We're meeting Terrell tomorrow after yoga. At least that's the plan. Woo Woo is going to call him tonight. We'll meet in the café and fill him in. That way we won't alert Jaxx, and the gym routine won't be interrupted with the arrival of a police officer.

I'm left with the feeling that we should be doing more, for Kristi, not the cop. There's something rolling around in the recesses of my mind, but I can't seem to pull it out. Must tell you about Charlene's condo though. It's quintessential accountant. You'd think a member of the LGBTQ+++ community would know better than to stereotype, eh. Nope.

It really is lovely. Bright, clean lines, aquamarine and white offset by pops of purple (like Charlene's hair). Even the dog had a turquoise bow tie. I don't think he liked it. On the other hand, he seemed to accept his role in the group with style: adore me, pet me, feed me. Repeat.

Madoff takes his job seriously. Good dog.

And there it is. That thing rolling around in the back of my mind. I'm going to be up for a while.

And I need to run to the store to buy doggie treats.

PS He came up in the conversation today about the watch. I think Nathan is going to be okay. I have to start calling him that. I have to accept he is real.

LH

Chapter 9.

The early morning sun is glinting off the Bedford Basin. Kristi doesn't notice it. What she does see are three students waiting for her in the entrance way: Lexie, Charlene, and Woo Woo. So much for a Zen-like state.

"Everything is okay. We have an idea – well, Lexie has an idea," Woo Woo says hurriedly. She can sense Kristi's trepidation.

Lexie lays out her idea. Clearly, she is excited. Charlene lacks the excitement but endorses the idea. "The sooner we can get this watch thing behind us, the sooner you can rebuild the business on a solid footing."

On the surface it seems like a simple idea, especially since Kristi doesn't have to do anything, and she thinks, "What harm can it do?"

They all agree that once Detective Terrell arrives Lexie will raise the idea, casually and offhandedly. Charlene wonders if these people have met Lexie. Woo Woo wonders if they have met Detective Terrell.

Lexie gives the class everything she has. She forces herself to be present and to go to her edge. The pose of the day is modified Marichyasana B, so no lotus pose is required, which is a relief. No way Lexie's leg is going to nestle on top of her thigh. Lexie gets further than she expected in the bind. She feels her hands are very close to touching each other. They aren't.

* * *

By the time Charlene and Lexie get to the café, Woo Woo has a quiet corner table staked out and a plate of pastries piled high. "She must have bolted from the room," Lexie thinks. Perhaps it has something to do with being excited about her idea. Charlene also marvels at Woo Woo's sprint from the studio but has no illusions about its impetus.

Bhodi and Honey have also joined the group today. Outsiders were to be expected. Terrell was requested to come 30 minutes after class, and he has been informed he may still have to wait until the others leave before finding out why he was invited to coffee. The plan doesn't go as expected, though. Honey sticks around longer than usual, and Terrell arrives early. Honey gives him a big smile. "How wonderful for you to join us," she says, and smiles at Woo Woo. Woo Woo turns her favorite color.

Terrell sits down and reaches for a pastry. "I need this. Long week."

It's not the time Lexie had planned to bring this up, but it is an opening as good as any. "I'm thinking about doing something new on my podcast. Would you mind if I run the idea by you?"

Charlene, Kristi, and Woo Woo respond enthusiastically. Terrell leans back and nods. Honey gives everyone a look. Charlene thinks she may have underestimated the farter.

Lexie lays out her idea. She wants to interview people in different jobs, in both senses of the word, get inside their profession. Understand what a typical – and an untypical – day looks like. Then she'll run a contest with listeners. They can create a skit based on what they've learned about the profession. There will be prizes. "I have lots of sponsors who will be willing to donate swag."

Woo Woo is the first to offer to be part of the podcast series. "Few people know what reflexology is. Who knows, it might even be good for business."

To Lexie's surprise, Honey offers to take part. "I hate to admit this," Lexie says, "but I'm not sure what you do."

Honey smiles and says evenly, "I'm the Associate Chief Justice of the Supreme Court of Nova Scotia." Lexie nearly falls off her seat; Charlene chokes on her raisin bran muffin; Terrell grins. This is turning out to be fun.

There's nothing for it. Lexie writes down Honey's name next to Woo Woo's. She looks at Charlene, who nods. "Count me in."

Everyone turns to Detective Terrell. He can't help it. He laughs. "Why the hell not."

Woo Woo claps. She just couldn't help herself.

Honey packs up five minutes later and waves good-bye to the group. Lexie feels she may have missed something here. "So," Detective Terrell asks, "what's up?"

"It may be nothing," Woo Woo says.

"Or it may be something," Lexie counters.

"But at some point, you will tell me what 'it' is," Terrell says. And Charlene does. She fills him in on the gym's financial state of affairs. Terrell listens without interruption. When Charlene has finished reviewing the handout (Detective Terrell got his own file folder), he turns to Kristi and says, "Why didn't you tell me before?"

Kristi hangs her head. Woo Woo pats her hand. Lexie makes a mental note to buy some moisturizer.

"I didn't know," Kristi says. She waits a second, looks up. "I suspected, but I didn't know. Now I do."

Charlene has outlined the steps Kristi and her new accountant have taken to stem the outflow of cash and stop the irregular bookkeeping. A copy of all the bank statements is in a thumb drive in Detective Terrell's folder.

"You know this isn't about the gym's money problems, right?" Terrell asks. He knows the answer but he needs to hear them say it.

Kristi speaks for the group. "We are all aware this may be a motive for Jaxx to steal the watch."

"Or you," says Terrell. He looks at her closely. Kristi has already been ruled out as a suspect because of the timing, but he is not sure she understands the full implications of what she has just been told.

"I was teaching a yoga class when the watch was stolen," she says simply.

"Yes," Terrell agrees, "you were. Your partner was not."

"Shit," says Lexie. "How did we miss that."

It is agreed that Kristi will go to the police station and give a formal statement. This is actually less agreement and more command. She will not tell Jaxx about her visit or that Detective Terrell knows about the money problems Vitality+ is facing. She will also not meet with Jaxx about this issue until Detective Terrell has spoken with him. He intends to do that tomorrow morning. This afternoon he will call Jaxx and request that he come to the station tomorrow for some follow-up questions. He wants him to stew overnight.

"What if Jaxx asks me what's going on?" Kristi says.

"Stay out of his way," Terrell says.

"We work in the same space," Kristi points out.

"Stay out of that space," the detective says.

Chapter 10.

Bitch. Jaxx twists the word around in his mind. Says it with silent ferocity. Greater ferocity, and eerie stillness. Then he says it out loud. He hisses – *"biiittchh"*. He spews the word into the atmosphere like a piece of bacon dislodging from a constricted throat. He slices the air with the word. It has become a machete. *"Bitch"*.

Jaxx doesn't remember ever having been this angry before. Then again, he's never been caught red-handed before. His charm, his lopsided grin, his easy good looks have always served him well. The benefit of the doubt has always been his. Until now.

Bitch.

At some point, Jaxx moves on to other words in the dictionary, two in particular: What Now. He knows he has been caught, and there is no coming back from that. The question is how to extricate himself from this mess with reputation and job intact. He's really not expecting much resistance. He can work Kristi into a little ball of contrition. Perhaps he might even have to turn on a little romantic charm. Wouldn't be the first time.

Jaxx starts to relax. The voice in his head, however, isn't done with him yet.

She went behind your back.

There is that, Jaxx acknowledges. The real question is whether she did this because he has lost control or because he didn't meet with her about the books. It's the latter, Jaxx decides. The voice in his head disagrees.

She involved other people.

That's embarrassing. Jaxx doesn't like to be embarrassed. Now he'll have to speak with those people or, more likely, get Kristi to tell them why they were wrong. All doable.

She stole the statements off your computer.

That is disconcerting, Jaxx admits. He didn't see it coming. Didn't think Kristi had it in her. Even if she got up the guts, she'd need support. The only way to get the bank statements was to hack his computer, and Kristi doesn't have those skills. She's got to have had help. But Kristi doesn't have a lot of friends. Jaxx knows. Could she have hired someone to hack his computer?

Think it through.

Jaxx tries breathing in for a count of four, holding for a count of five, and exhaling for a count of six. Something Kristi taught him. It works.

Odds are Kristi didn't have his computer hacked. I mean, how do you hire a hacker? Put an ad on Facebook Marketplace? The only other way to get the info would be to sit in front of his computer and download the files. But she doesn't have the password, and she couldn't guess it. Jaxx made sure of that.

Think it through.

So she couldn't get the info from outside the office, and she couldn't get it inside the office. The screensaver kicks in after two minutes. Shit. She had two minutes. But Jaxx would have to have seen her enter the office and he would have waited for the screensaver to appear.

Unless he was called away. That sometimes happens. One of the trainers needs something, there is a problem with the equipment, there is a potential new client.

Dammit.

The wingnut. Kristi had this whole thing planned out. She had been on to him for longer than he thought. That is his oversight. He got complacent. Still, he is a partner in the business, and he knows how to wrap Kristi around any of his fingers. He'll be all right, especially now that he has figured out everything that happened.

Jaxx finds himself smiling. He has worked through a difficult situation and come out the other side. He heads for the basement. Time to work out. This is how he celebrates, and how he copes. He steps on his new Life Fitness treadmill, compliments of Vitality+. Try downloading this, he thinks.

Jaxx is five minutes into what should be a 45-minute workout when the phone rings. He ignores the call until he looks down at the caller ID: Halifax Police Department. This dork again.

"Hello detective. How can I help you?"

"Wondering if you could spare some time tomorrow. I have a few more questions."

"I'll be at the gym at six." Jaxx grins.

"That's a little early for me." Terrell grins himself. "How about eight o'clock."

"See you then."

"Do you know where the main police department is in Halifax?"

"Can't we meet at the gym?" Jaxx knows something is up.

"It's probably better if we meet at the police station. "I'll see you tomorrow."

It takes Jaxx less than two minutes to think it through.

Bitch.

Chapter 11.

Jade is halfway through her 50-minute workout. Byron is across the floor with his personal trainer, the new one. The guy. And yet, he has his eyes riveted on her. Jade can feel his laser look piercing her skin, her thoughts, her organs. She admits she is being overly dramatic, but this is a daily ritual now. How to make the girlfriend feel inferior.

She's tired of it. Jade wants to be back in her office at the university dissecting reams of legal precedents. That, too, is dramatic, she concedes. There aren't reams. Still immersing herself in pollution is preferable to what she is doing now. More like where she is now: in a room with him.

Christian's dad is a small man. His insecurity drives him to push out his chest and pump his fists. At least metaphorically. That's what happens when you don't come from money. From status. You have to remind the world who you are. Jade knows who Byron Newhouse is. He's a mean human being with few redeeming qualities.

She does not doubt, however, that Byron loves his son. Doesn't make him a good parent, of course, but she can understand some of what he does to protect Christian and to make his life easier. That's what Byron thinks he's doing by driving a wedge between her and Christian. He'll get a girlfriend/wife/lover more in keeping with his stature.

Jade is sick of this crap. She is not sick of Christian though, so each morning she puts on workout clothes (from used clothing stores if only to drive Byron nuts) and meets Christian and his dad at the gym. She'd much prefer a yoga class, but Byron has already made a snarky and racist comment about her East Indian heritage, and she will not give him the satisfaction of thinking even for a second he is right.

The new treadmills come with consoles and Jade tries to tune in to whatever morning show is beaming from the screen. The hosts seem very happy. Jade invites them to spend the morning with her. They are talking about some new movie she will not see. Jade shakes her head and tries to focus on the conversation. She feels a new set of eyes on her.

Christian has come up behind her. He places a hand on the small of her back. "Are you okay?"

"I'm fine," she says, lying. He knows she is lying, and she knows he knows, but this is the safest way to keep the peace. Jade doesn't want to be the wedge that drives her and Christian apart. She wants to spend the rest of her life with this man.

Maybe Byron will die unexpectedly of a heart attack. Jade immediately regrets the thought. She wishes no one ill will, even Byron. Perhaps tolerance is part of her Indian heritage.

Christian is fussing with the water bottles. He hands her one. "What would you like to do tonight?"

"Absolutely nothing." Jade smiles. "Let's collapse in front of the TV with some wine and some Netflix."

"When did you get Netflix?"

Crap. She let that slip out. "I'm using a friend's license." Jade reaches for one of the water bottles. "Let's take advantage of it."

She knows they could always watch Netflix at Christian's place, or Amazon Prime, or Hulu, or any of a dozen other streaming services. But that would mean breathing the same air as Byron, and Jade doesn't have that much tolerance in her. She senses Christian's hesitation. She knows it is not because he wants to spend time with his dad (no one does), but because he worries about her. Now he is worrying she is paying for Netflix just for him.

They try not to make money come between them. Invariably, it does. Indeed, that's one of the reasons Jade is distracted, and a little distraught if she's being honest. She's worried the police detective thinks Christian stole the watch, and there is only one reason Christian would need to steal the watch: her.

It's why Byron detests her. She lives in the North end in a one-bedroom flat. She drives a seven-year-old car. She wears clothes other people have worn. Christian couldn't care less about her tax bracket, but he wants his dad to like her, and he wants her to have creature comforts. The stuff that matters to his dad and can make life more convenient and luxurious.

Byron keeps Christian on a tight financial leash, and that is okay for the most part. Christian doesn't want much, doesn't spend a lot. But he does worry about Jade and how Jade makes ends meet. She makes ends meet just fine, but Christian isn't convinced because she doesn't choose to live like his dad does, like his dad raised him to believe was the brass ring.

That is what is really bothering Jade, what has her on edge. It's not Byron and his dismissal of her as a human being. He is who he is, and Jade couldn't, quite frankly, care less, but she knows Christian cares, about her and about his father. How do you reconcile the two. One way: bring the two worlds closer together. How would Christian do that? Give Jade money she doesn't want or doesn't need. How would Christian get that money?

The answer to that question pierces Jade's heart more deeply than Byron's dirty looks ever could.

Daily Thoughts – Woo Woo
Monday, October 11th

I hate to admit I'm excited. It just doesn't seem right to be excited, but I am. Michael (everyone else calls him Terrell but he has a first name) wants Kristi and Charlene to go to the police station tomorrow to watch the interview with Jaxx. They'll be behind two-way glass. But Michael doesn't want Jaxx to know. He does want Jaxx to think Kristi is at the gym.

Lexie and Charlene will go in early to get the studio ready. Kristi will show up a few minutes before yoga class starts so Jaxx can't corner her. Jaxx will have to leave before class ends. Once he has left the gym, Kristi and Charlene will head to the police station. This is where it really gets exciting. I'm going to do a meditation for savasana.

I'm overflowing with ideas. There are so many options. I've narrowed it down to gratitude or compassion. Both are associated with the heart chakra, so I'll be sure to wear something green. I also have a green mat. I'll bring that. Ooh, I could put a drop of frankincense on everyone's third eye as the meditation starts. That would be fun.

I'll start putting some ideas down, but I don't want this to look rehearsed. I wonder if people in the yoga group will see me differently. Probably not.

And really, this isn't about me. Well, it shouldn't be. Kristi is beside herself. The business is in trouble, and her partner may be a thief. At the very least, he's an ass. I don't know what she's going to do, but Charlene will get her back on track financially. That will be a relief.

More exciting news. Lexie is doing a podcast about jobs – and I'm going to be a guest! There are three of us from yoga, Charlene, Honey, and me, plus Michael. I think I'll offer two lucky winners a free reflexology if they live nearby. If not, I'll offer a distance reiki. That would be great. Wouldn't it be something if Michael won.

I forgot the main point: the podcasts are intended to get info on the case. You know, the case of the stolen watch. (That would make a great title for a book. Or a movie.) Lexie thinks Michael might give us some insight if he's a little discombobulated being interviewed. I'm not sure discombobulated is in any of Michael's chakras.

But it doesn't hurt to try. Kristi needs our support. And I'll get to see Lexie's place. Bet it's all mismatched stuff. Maybe Ikea. Not that there's anything wrong with mismatched stuff or Ikea. It will be different from Charlene's place though. If this keeps up, I suppose I'll have to invite them over here.

I really don't want to do that.
You know why.
Sincerely,
Shondra Aeron

Chapter 12.

Terrell got up before his alarm went off at 6 a.m. He wants to be fresh for Jaxx Taylor. Usually, smug little bastards fall quickly and hard. But Terrell suspects Jaxx is smarter than less-pretty people give him credit for. If this guy stole Byron Newhouse's watch, he'll be on full alert and have already thought of ways out from under an accusation.

Coffee's on and Terrell grabs a cheese scone. (Woo Woo brought him a few to say thank you for coming to the meeting yesterday. Of course, it is his job.) The scone is very good. Terrell eats another. He makes a note to email Woo Woo a thank you.

He also makes a note to follow up with Byron Newhouse. Terrell is not surprised that Newhouse has not been nagging him, or his sergeant, for an update. Newhouse doesn't want the detective to make any progress. He thinks his son is guilty. Chances are he has also filed an insurance claim.

Robbery Homicide is on the fourth floor of the HPD building in north-end Halifax. There is a bullpen for detectives to work collectively (and the police department to save money on offices). This takes up most of the floor, at least what's visible, and the noise can be close to deafening when detectives are at their desks making calls, listening to interview recordings, and taking to each other and outsiders.

Lining the east side of the floor are six interrogation rooms, all with two-way mirrors. On the west side of the bullpen is the lunchroom and the crash room where detectives can grab a few hours' sleep (for those cases where overtime is approved). Terrell heads left. He makes his second cup of coffee of the day and pulls out a chair. He leans back and takes a tentative sip. Still tastes like crud.

The detective is in no hurry. He's told security to escort Jaxx to Interrogation Room 1 and leave him there. While Jaxx is cooling his heels and Terrell hopes building up a little heat, the detective waits for his other guests to arrive. After 15 minutes, Constable Reynolds sticks his head in the lunchroom door.

"You have company."

Terrell walks out to the bullpen. He reaches out a hand to Charlene Kurtz. She is unflappable. Kristi Yee is flapped. Terrell thanks them both for coming, trying to make the visit seem like a social call. Despite his warm tone, neither woman is buying what he's selling.

"Jaxx is already in an interrogation room, waiting. I'm hoping he's getting a little frustrated by now." Terrell looks at Kristi. She nods. "He is not a patient person."

"That's good," says Terrell. "You'll be in an adjoining room, behind glass. Jaxx cannot see you. But you can see him and hear everything."

Now both women nod. "I'm looking to you to tell me when the financial explanations don't make sense, and if Jaxx is acting out of character. I'll be wearing a coms set, so I can hear everything you say even though I'm not in the room with you. Constable Reynolds will be with you."

Terrell escorts the women to the listening area. He makes his way to Interrogation One and casually opens the door. "Sorry for the delay. Couldn't get a witness off the phone."

The detective grabs a chair on the opposite side of the metal table from Jaxx and swings it around so that he and the gym owner are sitting side by side. It's a standard interrogation technique. It's intended to throw people off. (Mission accomplished, Terrell thinks.) It also gives detectives a chance to look at a suspect's body movements up close and personal.

Jaxx is both disconcerted and exasperated. It's hard to say which emotion will win out. Terrell pushes him toward exasperation. "Tell me about your business. Specifically tell me why it's in financial trouble, and just how much trouble you're in."

The gym owner tries to look affronted and almost pulls it off. Terrell can see the muscles in his quads tighten, admittedly they are very well-defined muscles. "Look Jaxx. We can play this out if you want. You can pretend everything is fine. I'll haul out your bank statements to prove they're not. You can try to dismiss the discrepancies as no big deal. I can go through them one by one. In six hours, we'll be out of here. Or you can simply tell me what the hell is going on."

"How did you get my bank statements?" It is not a polite ask.

Terrell reaches for the intercom system sitting in the centre of the metal table. He presses a button. Constable Reynolds answers. "Danny, we may need lunch brought in. Just wanted to give you a heads up."

The detective turns to look at Jaxx. He takes his time. "I'm going to get us some coffee. I may even pick up some muffins. We're going to be here awhile. Sit tight."

Terrell walks out of the interrogation room into the observation room. He nods at Constable Reyolds who gets up from his chair and leaves. "He's going for coffee and muffins," Terrell explains to Charlene and Kristi. "He'll get something for all of you as well."

"He already took our order," Charlene says. "Are we really going to be here six hours?"

"Not a chance," says Terrell.

* * *

Jaxx takes a sip of the lukewarm coffee and grimaces. "How do people live like this?" he wonders. He thinks longingly of the Saeco espresso machine in his condo. That thought reminds him he charged the machine to the business. He looks up quickly and catches Terrell looking at him. The look is indulgent. You know, that look a parent gives a child who has been caught with their hand in the cookie jar. Jaxx responds with a look of his own: defiance.

"Now we're getting somewhere," Terrell thinks.

He waits a minute – and a minute is a long time when there is only silence and stillness. "I have a busy day ahead of me. I'm sure you do too. Let's cut to the chase. You have been taking money from Vitality+ illegally. Now, we can call it misappropriation of funds; we can call it embezzlement. I don't really care. I'm Robbery Homicide, not White Collar Crimes."

Jaxx senses an out. Perhaps he can still keep the cookie. Terrell waits just long enough for the gym owner to relax a little. "What I want to know is if you thought you could get out of your financial hole by stealing a very expensive watch. You know the watch I mean."

The statement is met with indignation. Terrell doesn't know if it's real or feigned. He waits. Jaxx denies ever taking the watch. "But you do admit to taking money?" Terrell asks.

"A little." Jaxx says reluctantly. "More than $300,000," a voice says in Terrell's ear.

"How much do you estimate?" Terrell asks.

Jaxx is smart enough to know he's trapped. The detective has the bank statements, although he's not sure how far back those statements go. At this point, he's decided to cooperate. If he can get the cop to ignore the money side of things, it will be worth it.

"I don't know. I'm telling you the truth."

Terrell believes he is. The detective sets the record straight. "More than $300,000."

The gym owner smiles. He's pleased with himself. He had no idea he'd gotten away with this much money.

"How long has this been going on?" Terrell asks.

"Since before we officially opened the business." Jaxx's smile is back.

Terrell can hear crying coming from the interview room. "A rose gold Nautilus would go a long way to paying some of that debt down."

"I have a plan for that," Jaxx says. "I'm going to open franchises. Bring in new investors. Expand throughout Atlantic Canada and then across the country."

Terrell scratches his nose. The voice in his ear tells him Jaxx is likely telling the truth. "How does Kristi fit into those plans?"

Jaxx shrugs. "She can keep the yoga studio, but I'll be going out on my own. Likely this year."

"Does Kristi know this?"

"She will." While helpful, Jaxx has just given himself and Kristi a reason not to steal Byron Newhouse's watch. Jaxx has bigger plans for his business, tarnishing its reputation does not make sense. Kristi didn't know about the expansion plans or the embezzlement, so no need for a watch and extra cash.

"Still, somebody stole the watch. You're looking like a solid suspect."

"I told you it was the little man himself. Or his son."

"We're looking into both those possibilities. If they don't pan out, we always have you."

"You've got a lot better than me," says Jaxx. Terrell waits. "The girlfriend is broke. She could use money." A grin hovers over Jaxx's mouth when he says "girlfriend."

"What's so funny?"

"It just occurred to me Christian isn't the only one with a girlfriend who has her hand out." Terrell doesn't have to wait. Jaxx is on a roll and he's picking up steam. "There was an incident in the gym a couple of weeks ago. Some blonde woman with big boobs and an even bigger mouth comes in looking for Newhouse. She let him have it.”

“What was the disagreement about?” Terrell scratches his nose. The voice in his ear tells him this is news.

“Apparently Byron likes to get his rocks off on a regular basis with women who aren’t his wife. He promises them the moon – and that he’ll leave his wife.”

“How do you know?”

“’Cause big boobs yelled it loud enough for me to hear, and I was in the office. Newhouse tried to calm her down and get her out of the gym, but she was having none of it. She told him to go fuck himself and stormed out.”

“I’ll need to corroborate this.” Terrell says as much to Jaxx as the constable and two women in the interview room.

“Ask Nathan,” Jaxx says. “He ran after her.”

* * *

Lexie has asked everyone to be at her house by 9:30. That will give her plenty of time to do the interviews before lunch and having everyone arrive at the same time gives Woo Woo and Charlene the chance to do some digging in the waiting room while Lexie is conducting an interview.

Nestled on the south side of a cul-de-sac in old Bedford, Lexie’s house looks a little like a cross between the gingerbread cottage in Hansel and Gretel and a cape cod beach home. A large deck extends off the side and around the back to a yard that borders a wooded area. Inside, the house is bright and modern with touches of memorabilia and the odd antique. Not what Charlene was expecting. Woo Woo thinks it's lovely.

The two women have arrived early to help Lexie set things up and review the plan. They realize there really isn't a plan, they'll be winging it, but there is comfort in numbers. The only thing they know for sure: Honey will go first (her request) and Terrell will go last (their idea). Coffee and tea (chai, green, and rooibos) are set out on the coffee table in the waiting room that adjoins the sound booth. Woo Woo has brought some homemade oatmeal cookies.

Honey arrives first, and she is joined almost immediately by Detective Terrell. They pour themselves a tea and a coffee, respectively, and reach for cookies. Plural. Lexie runs through how the interview will go, assures everyone nothing is live, and thanks them (again) for doing this.

Honey follows her into the recording studio, a small room with a bank of panels, knobs, and lights against one wall. A rectangular wooden table, maybe cherry wood, sits in the centre of the room. There are chairs on either side. In front of each chair is a large microphone with filter.

Lexie motions Honey to the chair on the furthest side of the table. "What would you like me to call you?"

"We probably shouldn't use Honey," the Associate Chief Justice says with a grin. "For official purposes, it is Justice Louise Redmond."

"Justice Redmond it is." Lexie skillfully leads Honey through a series of simple questions designed to make her profession and her day come to life. Lexie even gets in a few safe jokes; she'll edit it some more after the interview. Honey is ahead of her.

"My job is about respect and reverence, but there are very funny things that happen in a court room."

Lexie sits up. Who saw this coming? "Let's hear more."

"When I was a young lawyer, I was involved in a contract case. Both parties contended they were entitled to much more money than they had received. One of the parties was a very pregnant woman. As I was about to finish cross-examining her partner, her water broke and very quickly she was having contractions. I sat with her, helped with her breathing, and called for towels and hot water. I'm not sure why actually, but they do this on TV."

"If that's the punchline," Lexie thinks, "she shouldn't give up her day job."

Honey seems to have caught the quizzical thinking. She continues. "We had a long wait. Even paramedics can't just breeze by security in a courthouse. Finally, they arrived. It was too late. I was holding a bloody, screaming baby in my arms and everyone in the room was laughing, applauding, and crying."

"God, please don't let that be the punchline," Lexie says to herself. It isn't.

"About three days later I get a call from the woman. She's home. Baby's home. Everyone is healthy and happy. The woman tells me with pride that she has named the baby after me and every day she will remind the baby that her name is special because of the special circumstances in which she was born and the special woman who helped to deliver her."

"That's lovely." Lexie prepares to bring her guest back on track.

"It was," Honey acknowledged. "Unfortunately, she named the baby Lauren. My name is Louise."

Lexie hooted. Who knew judges were funny.

"I have a scenario for you," Lexie says. "Generalities. We'll be asking everyone how their profession could help in this situation."

Honey stiffens just slightly. Lexie continues. "Let's say there is a theft. Something valuable. Antique vase perhaps. Diamond bracelet. What does a judge do in this situation?"

Honey knows exactly what is going on here. Fact is, Lexie is not trying to hide it, and Terrell can't hear what is going on inside the booth, but everyone has to be asked or it will look like the detective is being singled out. "I'm the tail that wags the dog," Honey says. "Once the police have enough evidence to charge someone, or someones, the prosecutor reviews the evidence and decides whether to proceed or not. If the decision is to move forward, that's where a judge comes into the picture. Not me, mind you. I don't usually do criminal law."

"What does it take to convict someone?" Lexie pushes just a little. "Say someone was in the room at the time the crime was committed and knew the victim."

"Interesting segue," Honey thinks. "That wouldn't do it." Lexie swears Honey's shoulders relaxed. "That's circumstantial evidence and it usually doesn't hold up in court unless there is a lot of it. In the example you gave, it wouldn't hold up if there was more than one person in the room who knew the victim."

Lexie asks a few more questions but they are perfunctory. She's about to wrap it up when Honey unexpectedly says, "I do have an offer if your listeners are interested." She waits a second. "I got permission from my colleagues to have a listener shadow me for a day in court. They'll get to go back in the courthouse where the judges' offices are and sit up front with the bailiff during a trial. They may even sit in on some meetings with prosecutors and defense lawyers."

Lexie is thrilled. This will be good for the podcast. Mind you, the listener will have to be local. Lexie thanks Justice Redmond, and tells listeners there is more. She unveils the contest and refers everyone to her website for details.

Honey is already up and heading for the door. Lexie turns. "Thanks Lauren."

The next two interviews, Charlene and Woo Woo, go as planned. And not. Who knew Charlene was funny. She worked into the interview at least five jokes; two of them were amusing. Lexie's favorite: For every tax problem there is a solution that's straightforward, uncomplicated, and wrong.

Charlene also brought insight into the issue of theft and how accountants discover when a company's books are straightforward, uncomplicated, and incorrect. Likewise, she talked about how to find out if people have money problems. While it is difficult to access someone's income tax return or their credit card info, there are workarounds. Some of those, Charlene pointed out, are illegal, almost all are unethical. She called the latter loopholes.

In keeping with the tradition offered by Honey, Charlene offered to review someone's income tax return if they lived in Canada. For American listeners, she offered a free one-hour consultation, business or personal.

Woo Woo made reflexology sound normal. Like everyone does this. Woo Woo cited a study that found reflexology is the most popular complementary therapy followed by massage and aromatherapy. Lexie said she didn't like people touching her feet. Woo Woo told her to get over herself. Reflexology, she said, stimulates nerve function, increases energy, prevents migraines, and helps people sleep. Woo Woo said she would give Lexie a reflexology session on air, and she could share the experience in real time with her listeners. Lexie said, "Kinda like Jimmy Kimmel getting a colonoscopy on television."

Lexie thought this was a great line. Woo Woo did not. She did say though that she would contribute a free reflexology or reiki session to the prize pack. Lexie told listeners she would update the website.

Finally, it was time for Michael Terrell.

"It's important that you understand one thing about our next guest," Lexie says. "He's gorgeous. Dark brown skin, deep brown eyes, black hair closely shaven, and no hair on his face. "I'd touch it to see how soft it is, but there is something else you should know about Michael Terrell. He wears a gun."

This leads nicely into the intro of Terrell as a police detective. He gives some background on how he became a cop – wanted to help his community; loved the Mod Squad – and what a detective does. Terrell is trying to build bridges with listeners, many of whom are based in the U.S. where the laws and the lingo are different. He talks about gathering evidence objectively and exhaustively. It's like he's feeding right into Lexie's script.

"Let's say there is a theft, something valuable, how would you gather evidence?"

"If there is a crime scene, we'd start there." Terrell pretends this is a perfectly random scenario. "Someone may have left something behind, a fingerprint, a glove. It's not common, but it happens. I once arrested a guy for car theft. He left his application for McDonald's on the front seat."

"You must interview a lot of innocent people."

"I do." Terrell is not sure where this is going, so he takes the conversation in the direction he wants. "Interviews aren't just to find out who's guilty. They also help us find out what happened, how it happened, and who is connected to the crime.

"I'm in the middle of a case currently," he adds. Two can play at this game. "I can't talk about it specifically, but I will say lots of people were in the location at the time the theft occurred. They have all been very helpful. Some have even brought me homemade blueberry muffins." Woo Woo is in the waiting room listening to the interview. She turns her favorite shade of magenta.

That wasn't Terrell's intent, and it was. These women have to know he knows they are trying to get info out of him.

"Is there a usual 'guilty' party?" Lexie asks.

Terrell catches a whiff of hope. He gives her a quizzical look. Lexie refuses to meet his eyes. "Yes and no. The most obvious place to start is with people who know the victim well. This often gives them opportunity and motive. That said, the need for drug money drives many people to steal cars, break into houses, and mug strangers on the street."

Lexie pushes for a few more questions but really doesn't get anywhere. Finally, she thanks Detective Terrell. "Is there anything you have to offer for the prize package?"

Terrell grins. "I do. If your listener is local, they can touch my face. It's very soft."

Lexie and Terrell exit the recording booth. Woo Woo is standing in the doorway to the outer hall. "We have lunch ready," she says as if this was part of the plan all along. They walk to Lexie's kitchen nook, a lovely spot near the back door that overlooks the yard. The autumn leaves are out in full force and the sun is shining. "Glad the girls made themselves at home," Lexie thinks to herself. She can hear the snark in her own voice.

Charlene and Woo Woo have spread meats, cheeses, pickles, condiments, and at least three types of bread on the table. There are two containers of juice and a pot of tea. "Where the hell did all this come from?" Lexie wonders.

Terrell is also doing some wondering of his own. Time to end the charade. "This looks fabulous," he says sitting down. As he makes his sandwich – pastrami, smoked turkey, applewood cheddar, and bread and butter pickles – he says offhandedly, "Does anyone want to tell me what is really going on here."

Woo Woo turns magenta. Charlene examines a piece of black forest ham. Lexie steps up. "We don't really know. But we want to help Kristi. We thought if we knew where things stood, we would be in a better position to do that."

"So you want my job," Terrell says. Woo Woo and Charlene continue in their current states.

"Sure," Lexie says. There is that snark again. She skips a beat. "We know we aren't detectives, and we don't want to be. But we have skills, and we are at the studio five days a week. We see things."

Terrell's sandwich is now about a storey and a half high. He's trying to figure out how to bite it. "Okay."

Everyone looks at him in surprise. This is not what detectives say on TV. "I want to know a few things and you might be able to help." Woo Woo beams. Terrell beams back at her. "Get a room," Lexie thinks.

Lexie hands Terrell a knife, and he cuts his sandwich into four pieces. Problem solved. "I'm going to share some information with you, nothing confidential, but it will give you a sense of where the case stands. Hypothetically, of course."

The three women nod. "Let's say someone steals a piece of jewelry from a changeroom. The first issue is access. How does one get a watch, let's say, out of another person's locker?"

"You want us to try and get into the men's changeroom," says Charlene.

"I do," says Terrell. "This will put you in no danger, although it might prove embarrassing."

"We'll need to do it in the morning, when the watch was stolen," says Lexie. She starts thinking about the best approach. "This should work out well. It's Wednesday. That gives us three days to try and gain entry. We can each take a day.

"What else do you need?" she says turning to Terrell.

"I am making an assumption here," he says. Charlene swears he's blushing. "Women talk to other women, and to men. It's not gossip. It's chatting."

Lexie rolls her eyes. "What do you want us to chat about?"

"Byron Newhouse. Specifically, if he has a girlfriend at the gym, or elsewhere."

"What do you mean?" says Woo Woo.

"There is a suggestion Newhouse may have been fooling around. I'd like to verify that or confirm it is untrue."

"We can do that," says Charlene. She sounds sure of this. Lexie can't imagine Charlene in casual conversation.

"Anything else?" Lexie asks.

"I could really use some more of those homemade cheese scones."

Woo Woo beams. And turns magenta.

Daily Thoughts – Lexie
Wednesday, October 13th

The interviews were a success. Not exactly on topic, but there was plenty of humor to go around, and the contest is all about sending in the best punchlines, so listeners should be satisfied. I'm hoping they will be easier to satisfy than a room full of half-drunk people with no sense of humor. I'm approaching 3,400 downloads a month, which puts me in the top 10% of podcasts in North America. My bank account is happy. Very happy.

The cop also asked for our help. I'm not sure why. That would never happen on Law & Order: Special Victims Unit. Just sayin'. I don't think he's trying to pull one over on us. He just doesn't think this can do any harm. I agree. Don't see how it can.

One of our jobs is to "speak" with anyone who might have been around when the woman scorned showed up and tore a strip off Newhouse. Sorry I wasn't there. We decided I'd talk with Nathan. I said I knew him a little and he might open up to me. That's at least somewhat true. Charlene is going to seek out Ariel on the pretense of wanting a personal trainer. She can pull that off, and Ariel will have no option but to speak with her. She might not give up anything useful but there will be a conversation. Woo Woo is going to try and connect with Jade. This might be the hardest person to get talking. Woo Woo is just going to offer sympathy. Only Woo Woo could do this and have it work. She really does feel sorry for Jade and Newhouse's son. We'll try to get some traction on this tomorrow.

We were going to draw straws to determine what order we'd try to get into the men's changeroom, but then Charlene just decided. I should bristle at that. But the order is right: Charlene, Woo Woo, Moi. If we get caught, Charlene is going to be the savviest at talking her way out. I've dealt with hecklers on stage (nasty buggers), but it's not the same as being face to face with someone and having to explain why you're here. Charlene won't blink. Also, if she can get into the locker room and can steal something (that's our goal), then Woo Woo and I are off the hook. We'll know it can be done and relatively easily.

If Charlene doesn't succeed, Woo Woo is a good second choice. Especially if she wears that caftan thing. People don't expect logical explanations from Woo Woo. And the crimson wonder aside, Woo Woo is not easily embarrassed (unless you are a police detective who is also an African Nova Scotian god).

Me going third also makes sense. It will mean Charlene and Woo Woo failed. I'm more used to back rooms than they are, and I'm craftier. If any of us is going to get into and out of that room without being caught, it will be me. I just hope if I get caught, it's not Nathan who catches me. I'm sure he already thinks I'm a little strange.

If only he knew.

LH

Chapter 13.

Terrell thinks the women have a 50/50 chance of getting caught. If anyone can pull it off, he figures it will be Charlene. She's the most cautious, and to be a good thief, you need to err on the side of caution. People think it's about having guts and taking risks. It's really the opposite.

If no one succeeds, that likely means getting into the changeroom unnoticed is a very difficult thing to do. Failure would be a good thing, Terrell thinks. It would narrow the suspect pool substantially. The detective is not nervous about having asked non-law enforcement for help. Cops do it all the time, not on *Law & Order*, admittedly, but in the real world. Civilians can go where detectives dare not tread.

Constable Reynolds has tracked down the girlfriend, Abigail Downton. (Reynolds thought this was hilarious. Terrell doesn't get it.) Terrell plans to stop by her place after lunch. If she's not home – she is a make-up artist and often on set – he'll track her down at work, which he assumes will not go over well with her or her bosses. Nova Scotia is very protective of its film sector, the LA of the North.

First, though, Terrell heads to the gym. If this fight was such a big deal, how come no one has mentioned it until now. He catches Nathan as he's about to pack up for the day. Nathan clearly remembers the fight. He's uncomfortable just thinking about it, let alone talking about it. "She was really mad. Mr. Newhouse was really embarrassed. His son was there and heard the whole thing."

"Tell me about the 'whole thing'?"

"Oh man. I was trying not to listen. This woman shows up about quarter after eight. The gym is really full. There are lots of people trying to get in a session before work, and this woman storms in. She was livid. She goes up to Mr. Newhouse and starts yelling about having given him the best years of her life and giving him the best sex of his life, and he was never going to leave his wife. She told him to stay away from her."

"Did she threaten to tell his wife?"

Nathan thinks about this for a few seconds. "I don't think so. She seemed more upset about the floozy."

Terrell raises an eyebrow. "Yeah, that's right," Nathan says almost to himself. "She told Newhouse she knew he'd never leave his wife despite what he said, and that she could live with. But she wasn't going to play second fiddle to some tight-ass flavor of the month."

"Do you know who the flavor of the month is?" Terrell asks.

Nathan shakes his head no.

Kristi sounds as surprised to hear about the fight as Terrell was. "I certainly didn't hear any argument. It must have happened when we were down for coffee.

"Jaxx never mentioned it," she adds, "but then again we haven't been speaking all that often."

Kristi looks at Terrell trying to puzzle through what happened in her gym and why she's just hearing about this now – and what any of it has to do with the missing watch. Terrell sees the lightbulb go off. "She couldn't have been a member," says Kristi. "Jaxx and Nathan would know her. That means she wouldn't have easy access to the gym or the changerooms, even if she did have a copy of Newhouse's locker key."

Terrell is one step ahead of her. With a little help from the yoga tribe.

Abigail Downton is home. She doesn't seem the least bit surprised to see a police detective on the threshold of her condominium. "Abigail Downton?" Terrell asks.

"Abby," she says, ushering the detective in. (Ahh, now Terrell gets it.) "Took you long enough. I was expecting you several days ago."

Abby heads to a desk in the far corner of the room. Terrell takes a minute to look around. The condo, in downtown Halifax, is on the fifth floor and offers a stunning view of the harbor. A view like that doesn't come cheap, Terrell thinks. He glances around the room. Downton has obviously been relaxing. There is a drink, what looks like a mojito, on the glass coffee table and a book, *The Thong Principle*, with a bookmark sticking out. This room does not conjure up images of a screaming shrew, although the book looks interesting.

Abby is back and holding out a folder. She hands it to the detective. "This is what you're looking for."

Inside the folder are two pieces of paper. One is a deed of ownership showing that the condo belongs to Abigail Downton; Byron Newhouse has ceded title. The second is a printout of a bank statement showing a deposit for $125,000 from Newhouse. Both are dated for September 29th, two days after the argument at Vitality+.

"Not sure what I'm looking at," Terrell says.

"At least a million reasons why I don't need Byron Newhouse's damn watch and why I don't need to get revenge. I already have."

"How do you know about the watch?"

"Byron," Abby says simply. "He called to let me know you'd be dropping by. Didn't want another scene."

"Someone took the watch," Terrell points out.

"Probably the tart. Or Christian."

"Do you know who the tart is or where I might find her?"

"No idea." Abby starts to lead Terrell to the front door. He stops mid-route. "But you know there is a tart."

"Byron is a lot of things. Genius is not among them. Sent me flowers to thank me for a very special night. Only he didn't spend the night with me."

"What are the odds there is more than one tart?"

"Probably pretty good. But more than three women at one time? No. Byron doesn't have the brains or the cash flow for that."

"Can you tell me where you were ...."

"Yes, I can," Abby says before Terrell can finish. "I was doing make-up on the set of *Moonshiners* from 5 a.m. to 11:30 p.m. Then I came home to *my* wonderful condo."

Abby Downton's alibi will have to be confirmed, but Terrell has no doubt the make-up artist is telling the truth. After more than 30 years as a cop, Terrell can sense a liar before they open their mouth. Abby isn't lying. She's gloating.

Someone who won't be quite as happy about that failed relationship: Byron Newhouse. It's about 4:30 and traffic is heavy in Halifax as downtown commuters head home for the day across the Angus L. Macdonald Bridge and others cross town to the 102 to Truro and a myriad of other communities. Terrell figures Newhouse will still be at his office in the Burnside Industrial Park. He heads east across the A. Murray MacKay Bridge, what locals call the new bridge. Traffic is heavy but moving; an accident on the bridge can slow traffic to a crawl on both sides of the harbor for hours. Today, there are no snarls, pileups, or fender benders. In about 40 minutes, Terrell is walking through the front door of Bluenose Developments.

The company headquarters is in a commercial strip mall, standard fare in the park. The receptionist is gone for the day, but lights are on in the back. Terrell doesn't wait for an invitation. He walks toward the light. Newhouse appears to be the only one in the building. He's in an office with a large mahogany desk, bookcases along one wall and filing cabinets along another. In front of the bookcases is a blue couch that has seen better days and a faux-mahogany table.

"Sorry to interrupt," Terrell says without preamble. "I have a couple of questions. Won't take long." He clearly startles Newhouse who was preoccupied looking at what might be blueprints. This was worth the drive.

Newhouse collects himself quickly, but he does not come out from behind his desk or invite Terrell to have a seat. "Did you find the thief?"

"We're making progress. For instance, this afternoon I spoke with Abigail Downton." He waits for Newhouse to (a) get defensive or (b) give in to the inevitable conversation. "B" it is.

"That's private information."

"It may be information we keep from you, granted. However, Ms. Downton is free to share with us whatever she wants."

"Let me guess, she's a real sharer," says Newhouse with a sneer. He is confident either (a) Downton won't give the police anything of real value or (b) he can bluster his way through this. "B" it is.

"Mr. Newhouse, let me be blunt. Abby Downton strikes me as the type of woman who doesn't like her world rocked, unpleasantly at least. The police can be very unpleasant. There are interviews in interrogation rooms, numerous forms to fill out, more interviews, more forms. You get my drift."

"Serve her right." The thought seems to give Newhouse pleasure.

"She will, of course, need a lawyer," Terrell points out. "Not sure if she'll want to pay for that out of her own funds."

Newhouse opts for another multiple-choice answer. "What do you want?"

"Do you think Ms. Downton would take your watch?"

"No."

"Why?" Terrell wants to know. He also wants to know why Newhouse is still protecting this woman.

"Three reasons." Newhouse sits forward and starts counting on his fingers. "First, the watch has no sentimental value to me, so she wouldn't 'hurt' me if she did steal it. Second, she got more money out of me than the watch is worth – and with far less effort. Third, she couldn't get into the gym, the changeroom, or my locker without some real planning, a lot of luck, and a degree in criminology."

"Makes sense," says Terrell. Honestly. "Are there others out there like Ms. Downton with something to share who might not face the same obstacles?"

The developer sits back. Either this has not occurred to him or he is surprised it has occurred to a cop. "No."

"No, there are no other women out there I should be speaking with or no, there are no women out there who could more easily steal your watch?"

"Both," says Newhouse. "I'm done with women."

"And I'm done with breathing," Terrell thinks. He switches gears. "Have you filed an insurance claim?" Defensiveness radiates from Newhouse. This is a common reaction. "Not a problem one way or the other, but I have to note this in my report."

The developer seems to breathe a little easier. "I have been in touch with my insurance broker, but I don't know where things stand at the moment."

Terrell scribbles something in his notebook. Kinda looks like a muffin. "I'll also need the company's tax returns for the last five years."

Now Newhouse visibly bristles. "Why the hell do you need those?"

"Because you didn't tell us you gave your girlfriend more than $100,000 and a condo in the heart of Halifax."

"So what?" Newhouse says rising, literally, to the challenge.

"Mr. Newhouse, you're an intelligent man. You know that when a valuable piece of jewelry is stolen, one of the first avenues police will pursue is insurance fraud." The bristles are back. "I don't think you stole your watch," Terrell continues raising a hand to silence Newhouse. "I have to do my due diligence though. You would expect no less for your taxpayers' dollars."

Newhouse is appeased. Terrell and his colleagues learn de-escalation in their first year at the police academy. It's called Sucking Up 101.

"Trina is gone for the day. I'll have her send the returns over tomorrow."

Terrell is surprised at the acquiescence. So, Newhouse isn't hurting for money.

Chapter 14.

Charlene can't sleep. She knows it's nerves. At least that's what she keeps telling herself. Deep down she knows it isn't nerves at all. It's excitement. Not that auditors don't lead exciting lives, but Charlene is winding down her career. She didn't realize how much she missed having a purpose with some punch.

It's 5:30. Madoff is not pleased with being disturbed before the sun is up but graciously agrees to go for a quick walk and a pee. Well, several pees and a lot of sniffing. Madoff is surprised how many of his kinfolk are up and about this time of day. Charlene is less surprised, and more indifferent. She still has her pajama bottoms on. If anybody says anything, she'll pull a Woo Woo and tell them they are tulip pants. Whatever the hell they are.

Madoff takes a little extra time at the last hydrant, perhaps sensing something is up and it may be a while before he is anywhere near a tree. Charlene has both worked herself up and calmed herself down. She gives Madoff a hug. (A little too tight he thinks.) At home, before the pajamas are off and the yoga gear on, Charlene has texted Woo Woo and Lexie, suggesting they meet for an early coffee if they are up. The auditor is out the door before there is time for either to respond.

Lexie senses something is up when she reads the message. Early morning coffee is a first, so is the invite. "Why not?" she thinks. "I'll shower after yoga." By the time Lexie arrives at Muggs, Charlene and Woo Woo are well into their coffee and green pomegranate tea, respectively. There is a large cinnamon bun on the table, cut into quarters. One quarter remains. Lexie grabs a black coffee and sits down. "Everything okay?"

"Just nerves," says Charlene. Woo Woo pats her hand. When Woo Woo isn't looking, Charlene moves her hand into her lap.

"Glad you're up first," says Lexie. "If there's going to be hell to pay, glad it will be on your account."

"Now I feel better," says Charlene with a grin.

"I mean seriously, what can happen?" she adds. "We get caught in the men's changeroom. We apologize. Say we got confused. Swear we saw a mouse. Contend our ring rolled under the door. The worst that will happen is a bunch of people we don't know or care about will think we're a little strange."

"I know the feeling," says Woo Woo.

It's almost seven o'clock. Kristi likes to start yoga class on time. Charlene is debating whether to attempt the B&E before or after class. In the end, she does neither. It's what James Bond would do – the unexpected. She knows this because she has spent much of the night watching 007 movies. Judi Dench is her favorite.

Midway through a vinyasa flow, Charlene quietly excuses herself, taking her empty water bottle with her. The gym is busy but not crowded. She watches, surreptitiously, the men's changeroom door. Two men enter and exit a few minutes later. There is no other activity. Charlene bites the bullet. She saunters at what she hopes is a casual and nonchalant pace toward the changeroom door. She pushes on it.

Charlene is inside the men's changeroom.

It's disgusting. There are towels tossed about, water everywhere, and two pairs of very dirty sneakers sitting on the bench that runs in front of a bank of lockers. Something stinks. She's not sure if it's the footwear or the general aura of testosterone. Charlene makes her way quietly, à la Daniel Craig, toward a locker midway in the room. Any locker. Charlene feigns putting a key in the lock. She checks her phone. It has been two minutes and 12 seconds since Charlene entered. Piece of cake.

Charlene pretends to pocket the imaginary watch she has just stolen and turns to leave. Stealthily. She can't help but smile.

The naked man standing in the middle of the room staring at her, wipes that smile off her face.

Lexie can't stop laughing. She finds the whole thing hilarious and wonders how she can work this into a routine (the few she does each year) or her podcast. It occurs to her that maybe after this whole thing is over, she could do an episode, or several, on their adventures, and misadventures. Until then, Lexie continues to chuckle.

It takes Charlene a little longer to find the humor, but she eventually does. Woo Woo is looking for her hand, but Charlene has that tucked well out of sight. "He was buck naked. I mean just standing there dripping water everywhere. His mouth was hanging open."

"Bet that wasn't the only thing hanging," says Lexie, and bends over her chair in another spasm of laughter.

"What did you say?" Woo Woo asks trying to bring some decorum, and sympathy, to the discussion.

"Absolutely nothing," says Charlene. "I fled."

Lexie laughs so loudly the people at the next table openly stare.

* * *

Ariel needs a break. From work. From flabby men. From a boss who swaggers. She has vacation time left; what she doesn't have is money to spare. Personal trainers were hit hard in the pandemic as gyms around the country and the world shut their doors and clients went into lockdown. Even though Covid is in the rearview, Ariel's bank balance is still feeling the pain.

This was not supposed to be her life. By 30, she was supposed to be running a personal training empire from her home bases in LA, Phoenix, and Halifax. Still there would be time for the husband who adores her, and their two children, who also adore her. There is no empire. No adoring husband or children. Instead, there are two bedrooms in a 12-year-old apartment building in Bedford. The management company kindly sent everyone an email yesterday. Rent is going up. In January, Ariel will begin paying $2035 a month to not live in the lap of luxury.

The ex-boyfriend was helping. That was when he was the boyfriend. The prefix has done away with both the beau and his largesse. Ariel can ask her parents. She could also invest in cryptocurrency and become a billionaire overnight. The latter is more likely.

To add to her angst, there is the crap going on at the gym. Ariel assumes that has something to do with the semi-naked man standing before her yelling about a woman in the men's changeroom. She also assumes it may have had something to do with the yoga women hurriedly exiting the studio. One of them was laughing hysterically.

Ariel tries to calm him down. She explains that it is easy for new members to go into the wrong changeroom by mistake. Semi-naked loses a little of his huff. Ariel continues with the pacification. "Let us make this right. Please accept a complimentary session with one of the trainers."

Huff'n'puff is appeased. But he still has one last barb in him. "I don't care who sees me naked, but I do care about my belongings. You know there was a robbery here recently."

That fuckin' watch.

* * *

The women have decided they need to wrap up their efforts to penetrate the changeroom at Fort Knox (well, it's equivalent) before the weekend. That gives them one day: tomorrow. Yoga classes are offered on Saturday, but Lexie, Charlene, and Woo Woo (and they assume many of the other participants they know) do not attend weekend classes. Many of them go four or five days a week as the sun edges over the horizon. Come Saturday they are yoga'd out and ready to sleep in. Although they don't tell Kristi that.

That means Lexie, the final member of the triad to invade enemy territory, would have to attempt her entry on Saturday if they stick to a schedule of one person per day. They decide to change the schedule. This could be problematic if both Woo Woo and Lexie are caught on the same day in the men's changeroom, a day after another strange woman was found loitering here. Two women attempting entry would raise questions that one lone woman lost in testosterone country would not. Or it would raise questions that Woo Woo alone being caught would not, especially if she were wearing her harem sweatpants.

On the other hand, there is a different crowd on Saturday, so gaining or not gaining entry might not apply to the day Newhouse's watch got stolen. Also, because Woo Woo and Lexie are regulars they can blend into the background, familiar faces and all. They will stand out Saturday.

Two tries on Friday it is. Woo Woo will go first, before yoga class starts, and feign woo-wooness if caught. Lexie will go after class as the studio is emptying. If caught, well, who knows.

It is also decided to inform Detective Terrell about the success or failure of their missions right away. Woo Woo offers to invite him to coffee after class. Charlene thinks a text message would suffice but expects this is an option Woo Woo doesn't want to hear. Finally, everyone agrees another early morning meeting is needed to calm nerves, review options, and execute plans.

Charlene finds she's looking forward to getting up at the crack of dawn. Madoff does not share her enthusiasm.

* * *

Terrell orders a Propeller Prime lager from the tired waitress who is trying her best to be chipper. The detective hopes this is the end of her shift, not the start. He checks his messages and sees he has missed a call from Woo Woo.

"What are you smiling about?" says a voice at his elbow. It's a cross between a bark and a sigh.

"Nothing," Terrell says as his boss sits down beside him. He waves the tired waitress over. "She'll have the same as me."

"That better be champagne," says Inspector Jennifer Boone.

"You're lucky it's beer."

"This is what happens when you give police officers a ten percent raise. They get cocky."

"Have you seen the price of beer?" Terrell says. His boss laughs.

This is not a weekly or even monthly routine for the two officers, although it is not uncommon for them to get out of the station, review cases, and breathe a little more freely. Terrell has no problem with the fact that his boss is a woman, that she has risen through the ranks faster than he has (and faster than most men on the force). Truth is, she's a better leader. She sees beyond any single case to its implications for crime in the city, blowback on the force, and political interference.

Which brings them to the two cold lagers sitting on the pockmarked oak table. "It's a helluva watch," Boone says simply.

There is no need to ease into the discussion. Terrell knows why they are here, knows he is not in trouble, knows there is no pressure to close a case that isn't ready to be closed. And he likes a good craft beer. He also likes his boss.

"It is a very nice watch," Terrell agrees. "Apparently it is also a watch no one wants to fence. We've checked all the local pawn shops and dropped in for a visit with all the likely fences, even a few unlikely ones. No one has tried to get rid of the Nautilus 7010."

"That means this is personal."

Terrell nods. "Or our thief got scared and is bidding their time."

"Look at you with the gender-neutral pronouns."

"I am nothing if not woke," says Terrell. Few would know he is kidding. Boone is one of the few. She also knows something about this case is eating at her detective, a seasoned pro.

"What gives?"

"It's the last option that bothers me the most." Boone waits. "If our thief isn't looking for fast cash or a way to get even, they may be playing the long game."

"Shit," says Boone. "Just what we need. A smart thief."

* * *

Lexie sleeps like a log. The idea of getting caught doesn't bother her. You can't die of embarrassment. She knows.

As a stand-up comedian, there were nights she had audiences more interested in their cell phones than her set. Then there were the hecklers. The guys (it was always a guy) who wanted you to know you weren't funny. "Keep your day job." Lexie remembers one guy in Duluth (where the frig is Duluth?) who kept insisting she wasn't as good as his cousin, but she got to be on stage because she was gay. Lexie retorted, "Right, I dated her." That only set him off. It also set the audience off. Lexie tried to calm them down. "Don't worry about him. You can't cure stupid." There were nights she wished for an audience focused on their phones.

Being a comedian has taught Lexie to be fast, whether it's putting down a heckler or skewering with a quick retort. She's confident she can come up with an excuse for being in the men's changeroom if she gets caught.

144

Woo Woo does not share Lexie's confidence, but she's not worried about getting caught. Most of her life she has been the "different" one, the one who dressed a little out there, the one who had hobbies a little out there (and yet everyone wanted their tarot cards read). Woo Woo has learned to take this as a sign of living her truth. She is her authentic self.

Charlene says she doesn't know what that means. Woo Woo comes down to earth. She's been talking without being present. Woo Woo always tries to be mindful, but perhaps her mind is elsewhere. "Like coffee after yoga," says Lexie grinning. Woo Woo turns a lighter shade of plum.

Charlene has snagged the cozy corner and the three women are almost through their first cup of coffee and the array of muffins Charlene had ready and waiting for them. It's not even 6:30. "Well, that's decided then," says Charlene. "No decision needed about how to do this." Charlene doesn't like ambiguity. In auditing, every penny must be accounted for. It gives her a sense of satisfaction to know everything is in its proper place – or errors have been uncovered and corrected. Charlene is used to finding lots of errors.

"What if you get caught?"

"We've been through this," says Lexie, reaching for another muffin. "We won't go to jail. We won't be on the sex offenders' registry. We will, at worst, be embarrassed.

At best, we'll have helped the detective find out what he needs to know."

Lexie looks at Woo Woo, still glowing a muted crimson. "You know," she says, "there is such a thing as spontaneous combustion."

Yoga class starts in 10 minutes, more than enough time for Time Flies, as Lexie has dubbed the undercover op. She really does watch too much television, Woo Woo thinks. The other women have gone into class; Woo Woo is hovering by the water cooler pretending to fill her bottle. There is a steady trickle of men in and out of the changeroom. The trickle seems to end, and Woo Woo makes her move.

She heads quickly to a locker and pretends to open the door. She mimes reaching inside and removing a watch. She envisions herself putting the watch in her pocket. Visualization comes easily to Woo Woo. She meditates every morning. Many of those meditations are guided visualizations. This is going so much better than she anticipated. Woo Woo pats her pocket and the imaginary Patek Philippe.

"What the hell are you doing?" Jaxx asks, and none too nicely. Woo Woo swirls and comes back to reality. The gym owner is standing three feet from her with a stack of clean towels in his arms.

Everybody knows about the flight or fight response. They don't usually know there is a third option: freeze. Woo Woo opts for the last one.

"Yo," says Jaxx, waving a hand in front of her face.

"Where am I?" Woo Woo asks.

"The men's changeroom. Where did you think you were?"

"Sorry," says Woo Woo. "I must have been astral projecting."

"Get out," says Jaxx. He points to the door. Woo Woo makes her way across the room. She makes sure he can't see her smile.

Yoga class is just about to start when Woo Woo walks in. She shakes her head no. Kristi has no idea what she's doing. Lexie and Charlene do.

"It's down to me," Lexie thinks. She likes a challenge. Perhaps that's why she likes comedy, even though it can be a tough profession. The travel, the beige hotel rooms, the deep-fried meals. The sound of applause.

Lexie thinks of that as she stakes out the changeroom. She also thinks, yet again, she may watch far too many cop shows. There's a whole bunch of sweaty men in the gym working out. If they're out here, they're not in there, Lexie surmises. Figures now is as good a time as it gets. She walks into the changeroom without hesitation. Confidence is everything on stage. Last night Lexie ran through a skit where someone steals a watch. All she needs is, at most, 78 seconds.

At 46 seconds, Lexie feels someone tap on her shoulder. She turns around and trips into Nathan's outstretched arms. "Are you okay?" he asks.

"No," Lexie thinks. "I am not okay." She looks at Nathan. She turns Woo Woo's favorite shade. She takes a page out of Charlene's playbook. She flees.

Stupid. Stupid. Stupid.

Charlene and Woo Woo are waiting in the coffee shop for Lexie and Terrell to arrive and for what they hope will be good news from Lexie. Perhaps she can pull it off. It's almost 9. The work crowd has already picked up their coffee and the yogis have left to begin the rest of their day. This meeting was set for later, so they would have privacy and no other company. The corner sofa and chairs are scattered with yoga mats and water bottles. Empty coffee cups sit on the table. Charlene goes for refills. She breathes in the aroma of roasting beans. It's one of her favorite smells, bringing back memories of early mornings with her father. He would drink his fresh-brewed coffee while he made her toast with a banana smile.

By the time Charlene loads up on coffee and treats (she opts for lemon cookies), Terrell is at the table. He's smiling. Woo Woo is beaming a purple haze. The atmosphere is about to splinter. Everyone knows something is wrong as soon as Lexie enters the coffee shop. She tries to shrug it off. "Got caught. No big deal."

Terrell has seen enough upset witnesses. He knows when it's time to let them compose themselves. He gives Lexie that time. The detective turns to Charlene and Woo Woo, who is about to reach over and pat Lexie's hand. She catches Terrell's look and pulls back.

"I take it we're three for three," says Terrell. Woo Woo thinks that might be a sports reference. She wonders what sports Michael likes to play and thinks perhaps she should watch a game of something or other on TV.

The women nod, not sure what comes next or even who should speak. Lexie decides for them. "You'd have to be damn lucky or damn smart to get the watch out of the changeroom without getting caught."

Charlene is calculating odds. "That means it's not likely random."

Terrell nods. "It actually means more than that."

The three women look at him. "It means whoever was in that room and stole that watch had a right to be there. They would not stand out."

"Oh my God," says Charlene, calculations complete. "Whoever took the watch is a gym member or an employee."

Terrell nods. Lexie turns a whiter shade of pale.

Chapter 15.

Nathan shakes his head as if to clear away fog. He's not sure what just happened in the changeroom. That is not an unusual state for him, especially when it comes to women. Not that this woman is a woman in the sense of "women." Nathan shakes his head. He's not making sense even to himself.

The personal trainer heads to the gym floor. He has a client in 15 minutes and needs to get some gear ready. This client is not serious about getting fit, but he's serious about being seen to get fit. Hiding behind gear works for him if not his heart.

Lots of clients are like this. They have the best of intentions but no commitment. Nathan isn't sure how to build commitment, and he has been doing this for a decade. He looks at the yoga studio and the people who seem to come regularly, some every day, like the woman in the men's changeroom. Lexie. She has introduced herself. That was a little strange Nathan used to think. Now she's just a familiar face.

Nathan is convinced, or has convinced himself, she is not interested in him romantically. Or sexually. God forbid.

Anyway, she's gay. Nathan knows this because he has listened to her podcast. It's very good. Nathan doesn't have the ability for a quick retort, and he doesn't like being centerstage. Lexie has done stand-up. Nathan could never do that. All those people looking right at you. It's okay when it's one person and they're sweating. Well, not that kind of sweating.

Nathan wonders if reticence might be learned. His adoptive parents – wonderful people whom he loves to death – are confident and kind and thoughtful, but they are not charismatic. He has followed in their footsteps, or perhaps these are his genetic footsteps. Either way it means Nathan will not be pursuing a stand-up career and he will not be chasing after Lexie to find out why she was in the men's changeroom. Perhaps it's a bit for her podcast.

Bet that's it. Who knew Nathan would be part of a bit.

* * *

Kristi is ready to confront Jaxx. It's time. The business is at stake and her peace of mind is already fractured. Confrontation does not come easily to Kristi. Perhaps that's why yoga is so appealing. It is the antithesis of competition, condemnation, and conflict.

Even as a young girl growing up in Toronto, Kristi preferred the quiet of the shadows to the glare of the spotlight. Kristi is not a glarer. Once in the school gymnasium another girl hit Kristi with a volleyball. They were not playing volleyball at the time. Everyone knew it was deliberate, including the teacher, Ms. Franklin. She asked Kristi if there was anything she wanted to say to this other girl. Kristi nodded no. She kept her eyes on the floor. The other girl smirked. Kristi can't even remember the kid's name, but she has never forgotten that feeling. Something tells her she is going to experience that moment all over again tonight.

She told Charlene and Woo Woo her plans over coffee. As usual, they supported her. They offered to be there with her, but Kristi has decided this is something she needs to do herself. She needs to take her eyes off the floor. Jaxx is coming to her place. Kristi remembers reading somewhere that you have the upper hand in a negotiation if it is conducted on your turf.

Kristi's turf is a lovely two-bedroom apartment about five minutes from the studio. She pays $1,800 a month, more than she can really afford but she justifies the expense by telling herself she saves on gas, improves her health walking more, and is reducing her carbon footprint. If the business is mired in trouble though, Kristi may have to look for more affordable accommodations. She knows there is no such thing in Halifax.

Usually if Kristi is having company, which sadly she admits is not often, she would serve some wine and cheese, or fruit and sangria, something festive or appetizing. She's not sure her meeting with Jaxx is that kind of occasion. She calls Charlene. Auditors are good with conflict and tension.

"No treats," says Charlene. "Offer him a cup of coffee or tea. Water. Have the table ready and papers spread out on it."

The table is ready, the French press primed, and a carafe of water in the fridge. It's seven minutes until seven, Jaxx is never on time. Kristi decides to go through a few Vinyasa flows to keep her focused and calm. At 7:15 her intercom rings. Jaxx is on his way up.

Terrell looks around. He's trained in observation. He takes in the modern art rug that spans the length of the corridor: black, grey, charcoal. Contemporary and functional. It will be hard to find dirt on this carpet. The walls are a paler shade of grey with maybe a hint of mauve. His oldest sister would probably call it lavender. She watches the Property Brothers.

It's been a while since Terrell has done surveillance. That's what this is. You can call it something else: doing a favor for a friend, helping out someone going through a hard time, gathering background on a suspect. But it's surveillance.

The detective has come prepared. He has a bag of snacks – overflowing with gluten, dairy, and processed sugar. His phone is fully charged and loaded with games. He even has an empty water bottle in case he needs to.... Well, you know.

Terrell checks his watch. It's 7:20. Whatever is going on inside Kristi's apartment, all is quiet for the moment. Terrell hopes it stays that way. He knows Woo Woo and her friends are worried about Kristi. He knows that because Woo Woo told him when she called in the middle of his reheated Sobey's mac and cheese.

She apologized for calling as only Woo Woo can, Terrell is discovering. He knew before she finished her first sentence he would be doing whatever she needed. Indeed, he offered. Woo Woo didn't have to ask. She had him at hello.

So here he is sitting on a charcoal rug playing a vintage game of Candy Crush, eating a KitKat, and straining to hear what's going on behind closed doors. All is quiet on the western front.

Terrell takes a minute to reflect on how the hell he got here. Perhaps there is something to this yoga, meditation, reflexology stuff. Perhaps he should give it a try. No time like the present.

The 6'2", 55-year-old Detective First Class stands up. He puts his back to the wall, legs bent, and begins to slide down. He saw the class doing this the first time he went to the yoga studio. It's like sitting in a chair without a chair. Seems to Terrell the yoga students bent a little deeper in their invisible chair. Terrell tries to bend deeper. Nothing happens. That's not true, he discovers. A sharp pain travels up his quadricep and takes aim at his groin. Terrell tries to stand up. Still nothing happens. Yoga is taking on a new perspective.

Knees bent, slightly, back against the wall, shoulders back(ish), Terrell tries to figure out how to get out of this shape without more pain. It occurs to him that he could straighten one leg, then the other. Now it's like he's half lying down. He brings his outstretched legs back to the wall and stands up.

He can hear movement inside. He moves closer to the door. Perhaps chairs scraping. Into the table or away from the table?

In the silence that follows, Terrell heads back to the wall. He's ready to try another pose: tree. He saw everyone doing this when he was doing interviews. He faces the wall and brings his left foot to rest against his right ankle. Piece of cake. Terrell raises his foot to his upper calf, a small twinge of tightness, but the detective is pleased with his flexibility and balance. He raises his hands to the wall and breathes for a count of five. Now he lifts his foot to place it against his inner thigh. His foot refuses to cooperate. This can't be right, Terrell thinks. He tries again. His foot falls to the floor.

Terrell decides to try the other side. (In yoga, he has learned, balance is critical.

What you do to one side of the body, you do to the other.) Ankle. Check. Upper calf. Check. Inner thigh. Not a chance in hell. Terrell looks down at his thigh, then his foot. This can be done, he thinks. Terrell grabs his foot and inches it toward his thigh. It never gets there.

Kristi's door flies open and Jaxx – red-faced, furious, and running on full steam – charges out. "Screw you, bit..." Jaxx stops mid-expletive. He spies Terrell hugging the wall, his foot dangling toward the floor. Jaxx closes his mouth and storms off.

Kristi is at the door now. She sees Jaxx in the corner of her eye, but she is looking straight ahead at the man ahead of her trying to do tree pose. Terrell tries to lower his foot. It has fallen asleep. Terrell lands on his ass. Kristi reaches out a hand to pull him up.

"Are you okay?"

Terrell nods. Kristi breaks into tears.

With a sobbing yoga instructor in his arms, Terrell does the only thing he can do. He texts Woo Woo. Woo Woo calls Charlene, and Charlene calls Lexie. Now everyone is in Kristi's apartment (which Charlene thinks speaks well for the business and the tenant). Terrell has given up on finding anything remotely resembling coffee or beer. He's put a selection of herbal teas in a bowl on the glass dining table. (He remembers his mother doing this when they had company.) Woo Woo gives him a broad smile, and Kristi says thank you. Silently Lexie mouths, "Coffee?"

Terrell shakes his head no.

By now, Kristi has calmed down. She is moving from being upset to embarrassed. She doesn't want the world to know her problems, even if that world is full of supportive friends and one police officer with remarkably well-defined arms. Charlene et al are having none of this. Woo Woo pats Kristi's hand, and Charlene asks what happened. It's what everyone wants to know but no one had the nerve to ask.

"Jaxx says if I don't give him back access to the books and the gym's finances, he's leaving. He says I'll have to buy him out of the business. I don't have that kind of money." Kristi starts to cry again, wracking sobs that physically move her body. Lexie reaches over and pats her hand.

Everyone looks at Charlene. It is a look the auditor is familiar with. Even before she had her CPA designation, people turned to Charlene for answers to often complex questions and not always financial. This question, however, is in her wheelhouse.

Charlene takes a sip of her honeybush and mandarin tea. She enjoys being the expert, but she is finding she enjoys being a friend a little bit more. She wants to answer this question so it is both factual and hopeful. "I'd have to read the terms of your agreement, but my guess is you both have an exit clause and a buy-out clause. That protects both of you from having to stay in a business you no longer want to be part of and from losing a business you love."

"So Jaxx is right," Lexie says. Kristi continues to cry softly. Charlene wishes she could cry like that. Very delicate. What her mother would call ladylike.

"Jaxx is right, and he's wrong," says Charlene. That gets everyone's attention. "The business has a certain value, and if you both own half the business, Jaxx is entitled to his half. However, businesses also have debt, and the debt has to be paid off first. Or in your case, deducted from the value of the business."

"What does that mean for people who don't speak balance sheet?" Lexie asks. Sometimes she misses stand-up.

"It means that Jaxx would likely be entitled to very little cash. We know that the company is in trouble. What we don't know is if Jaxx has benefited directly from the financial mismanagement. If he has, he'd have to pay that money back first or it would have to be deducted from the value of the business."

Charlene feels three sets of eyes on her. "I doubt Jaxx would get a cent." Kristi puts her head on her arms and sobs. Charlene knows too much hope can be a dangerous thing. "In my heart, and in my experience, I know Jaxx has taken money from the company and used it for himself. But I can't prove that. He could bluster his way through this."

"How do we suck the bluster out of him?" Lexie wants to know.

"We need proof he has stolen money or equipment," says Charlene. "The threat of legal action, especially a charge of fraud, is often enough to get people like Jaxx to back off."

Now everyone is looking at Terrell. He's leaning over the tea bowl trying to decide between an apricot amaretto and a white chocolate raspberry. There's also a vanilla rooibos, but he is not sure what rooibos is. Perhaps Kristi would let him take home a few to try. It's not the piercing eyes that stop Terrell's search for the perfect brew but the silence that has descended. He looks up.

Woo Woo smiles encouragingly. Lexie tilts her head. "So?"

Terrell hesitates for just a second. "I'll need a little more."

"Can you prove Jaxx is a thief?" Lexie asks.

Daily Thoughts – Charlene
Friday, October 18th

It's been a full day. That is a good thing. And maybe not. The big news, I guess, is that Jaxx may be leaving the gym business. That would be good for Kristi. I mean he'd be gone. It might not be good for her money wise. Even if she doesn't have to pay Jaxx anything, she still has a business mired in debt. That is rarely an easy pit to climb out of. (Is "of" a dangling preposition?)

We haven't really talked reality with Kristi. Tonight was just too raw and too emotional – and too unexpected. I don't think Kristi thought Jaxx would pull out. Certainly, none of us thought we'd end up at Kristi's for three hours. Madoff was not happy. I gave him a piece of Woo Woo's gluten-free pumpkin muffin when I got home. That seemed to appease him.

I'm still not sure how we ended up at Kristi's. Woo Woo called me. Apparently the detective called her. But what was the detective doing there? I thought he was more interested in Woo Woo. It's all so confusing and disconcerting, and I'm sitting here in my comfortable Perry chair (I got it on sale) with a sleeping dog in my lap and a half-eaten muffin. If I'm disconcerted, what in heaven's name is Kristi feeling.

We've agreed to reconvene tomorrow. Terrell has offered to help us find out if Jaxx is stealing. Even though tomorrow is Saturday, Terrell is going to visit Jaxx at his house – Kristi says it's actually a good day, Jaxx is more likely to be at home – and poke around. I told him to get pictures. If he's stealing equipment, we can match it against the purchase orders and receipts.

We're going to meet at Woo Woo's for lunch, and it's about time if I do say so myself. We've been to my place and Lexie's place several times already. Now we've even been to Kristi's. Woo Woo has to know we don't care if she doesn't have a lot of money (not that we have a *lot* of money). I think we're becoming friends. We have to move past this. I'll bring some biscotti to have with our coffee.

I'd like to have a cup of coffee now, but it would keep me up all night. I might be up anyway. About three minutes after I got home, and four seconds after Madoff inhaled most of my muffin, Dora called. She assumed I would be home. I wish I had gotten home ten minutes later.

I love my daughter, but her assumptions of my life can be grating. Usually because they are right. We talk about the weather and yoga class and my consulting work. That usually eats up five minutes, then we struggle. I never struggle with Billie. Conversation comes naturally. Of course, she is the controller for an oil company in Alberta, so we can talk about her work and the economy. Truth is, I don't have much in common with Dora. She's curator of a modern art gallery in Vancouver. I don't understand modern art. She obviously takes after her jazz musician father.

To her credit and mine, we try to find common ground. Invariably the terrain is rocky. Dora is still on about that ancestry thing. It was my Christmas gift last year. She even walked me through the registration process. If it were up to me, I would have regifted it. I don't care about my family history. I know who my mother is and my father. A few aunts and uncles, a smattering of cousins. I'm good. But Dora pushes.

Now she has pushed me to him. He's called again. Says he won't bother me anymore but is hoping we can connect. I'm hoping we don't. Perhaps I should ask Woo Woo and Lexie what they think.

It's really all too much. First, we need to help Kristi through this rough patch. Then I'll deal with my problem.

You can't see this, but Madoff has now dragged his dog bed into the middle of the living room. That means it is time to call it a day whether I'm tired or not. But Madoff is right. A good night's sleep – if I'm lucky – will work wonders.

Sincerely,

Charlene Kurtz

PS I have a strange little thought rolling around in my head. Could be a great idea. I'll need Lexie and Woo Woo though. Or it could be I'm overtired. Madoff's right. It's time for bed.

Chapter 16.

It's 8 a.m. It's Saturday. It's overcast. It's perfect.

Often the best way to get information out of someone is to catch them off-guard. Terrell figures Jaxx either had a night on the town following his confrontation with Kristi or he had a lousy night's sleep. Or both. All of which is good news for getting inside his head and his condo.

Terrell rings the doorbell and waits. And waits. Terrell rings the bell again. And waits. It's a game of persistence. Terrell wins. It takes Jaxx 10 minutes to get to the front door, throw it open and yell, "What the f..." He stops mid-profanity when he sees Terrell.

"Oof, rough night," the detective says as he gently pushes Jaxx aside and steps into the entrance hall. "Thank you. I'd love a cup of coffee."

The gym owner gives up in defeat and heads up a small flight of stairs to the kitchen. Terrell heads to the basement calling over his shoulder. "I'm going to the can. Be right up."

It takes only a few minutes to snap pics of the seemingly new gym equipment that takes up most of the downstairs. A small bar with a few cozy chairs are the only other furniture and pieces in the basement. Terrell heads upstairs after flushing the toilet.

Jaxx has a cup of steaming coffee in front of him and another is brewing. Since Jaxx is sipping from the full cup, Terrell assumes his coffee is the one now hissing out of a very sophisticated machine. "Smells great," Terrell says to a clearly disgruntled Jaxx Taylor.

Terrell walks through the kitchen and into the living room, which has a fabulous cream-colored sectional sofa that wraps itself around the room. Footstools and coffee tables are strategically scattered at right angles. "Nice place." Terrell takes out his camera and snaps a few more pics.

The movement does not escape Jaxx's notice. "Hey. What are you doing?" He moves forward as if to stop the detective. Then he looks at the detective. Jaxx stops mid-stride.

"Thinking of redoing my place," says Terrell. "Doubt I could afford this though."

The implication doesn't go unnoticed. "Screw you," says Jaxx. "I'm allowed to own furniture. And you need a warrant."

"For what? Coffee?"

"Did you just drop by to admire my sofa or is there a reason you're here in my house at this ungodly hour?"

"Right," says Terrell. "I'll be in the gym on Monday morning, specifically the changeroom. Wanted to give you a head's up."

Jaxx rolls his eyes. "What are you going to do? Sit on a bench for an hour."

"Yep," says Terrell. "Great coffee." He puts his empty cup on the granite countertop and turns to leave. He takes a picture of the Saeco espresso machine on his way out.

* * *

Woo Woo is worried about lunch. Well, not about lunch. Lunch is lovely. She's got meat, cheeses, veggies, hummus, tzatziki and other dips, pickles, and an assortment of bread and rolls. Everyone can make their own sandwich. For dessert, she's made thumbnail cookies and brownies. Comfortable and comforting, she thinks.

What's worrying Woo Woo is how her new friends, and she has come to think of them as friends (well not Michael, of course), will react to her house. Woo Woo loves her house. She has filled it with images of bees and Buddha, flowers, and flea market finds. She thinks it feels like her on the inside. But she knows it will not be what her new friends expect, and she doesn't know them well enough to know how they will react. She's about to find out.

Lexie is not great with directions. She has GPS in her car, Google Maps on her phone, and instant access to Siri. Still, she knows she can get turned around, lost, and misdirected at the drop of a hat. According to the address, Woo Woo lives on Shore Drive, an exclusive Bedford community that hugs the Bedford Basin and offers stunning ocean views. Lexie knows this really means Woo Woo lives in the townhouses at the end of DeWolf Park, which connects to Shore Drive. DeWolf is a popular spot for joggers, dog walkers, toddlers on leashes, and picnickers. Parking is easy here, and free, although it means Lexie has to walk.

She heads west. Or maybe it's north. Well, it's left. At the end of the boardwalk are several rows of townhouses, perhaps they're called cul-de-sacs, Lexie thinks. She assumes Woo Woo lives here. It's a lovely neighborhood. Lexie makes her way to the first row. (It's hard to get lost. It's a straight line.) There is no obvious street sign, but the townhouses are visible.

Lexie is looking for 1A Shore Drive. (She wonders what the "A" stands for.) Of course, there is no 1A. The townhouses all have numbers in the hundreds. Lexie heads to the next cul-de-sac. Not a 1A in sight. She stops a woman walking a dog about the size of a guinea pig and asks for directions.

"Shore Drive is over there," the woman says pointing to a trail that connects to the park. Guinea Pig cocks a leg in agreement.

Lexie knows what comes next. She goes to the trail. She gets lost. She asks someone else. She ends up back here standing in

Guinea Pig's urine. But it's the journey, not the destination, right.

At the end of the trail are three huge homes that have been years in the building and just as many years mired in controversy. Lexie (and most of the other DeWolf visitors) remember when the for-sale sign went up. The cost: $1.6 million for the land alone. Lexie hasn't seen the houses since they've been built, so maybe the walk is worth it after all. She's curious what they'll be like, perched on the edge of the Bedford Basin, a stone's throw from the water that defines Halifax's history, its present, and its future.

The first house is a large, well huge, three-storey house that consumes at least an acre of land Lexie figures. (She's not sure how big an acre actually is.) What Lexie notices most about the beautiful home though is its address: 1C. In behind are the two other estates, one a long modern home that has rows of windows on both sides. On the roof: solar panels. A meandering walkway leads to the front door, where a sleeping Buddha silently welcomes visitors. Above Buddha's slumbering frame: 1A.

Lexie is too busy being stunned to hear Charlene come up behind her. She does feel Charlene's hand on her shoulder though and nearly jumps through the slate roof. Before Lexie can say anything, like "Who knew?" or "WTF?", Woo Woo opens the door and ushers them in.

"Welcome."

Charlene glances around the house with its open concept, eggshell background, cherry wood paneling, and profusion of bumblebee motifs. They're even on the legs of one sofa. "It's lovely, Woo Woo."

"Reflexology obviously pays well," says Lexie.

"Not that well," says Woo Woo. "This is family money." She hears the unasked question; she's heard it her whole life. "My last name is Aeron."

That means nothing to Lexie. It means something to Charlene. "Good God, you're Aeron Aerospace."

"I'm not," says Woo Woo. "My dad is. My very generous dad."

"Would he like more kids?" Lexie asks.

Woo Woo takes them on a tour, downplaying the custom tile flooring, marble countertops, and temperature-controlled wine room. When they're back in the kitchen, she offers up spritzers, tea, juices, and more.

"Can I move in?" Lexie wants to know.

Woo Woo isn't sure whether to cry or laugh. Money changes everything. Charlene answers the question for her. She chuckles at Lexie's joke, and just like that Woo Woo is one of the girls again, albeit with a bigger wallet.

Terrell and Kristi show up about fifteen minutes later. (Woo Woo gave them a different time to arrive.) By then the three women are enjoying a glass of Tidal Bay and trying to guess what the detective has uncovered. Kristi says nice things about Woo Woo's home (Kristi is always nice), but you can see her mind is elsewhere. Terrell lets out a low whistle. Woo Woo takes it as a compliment.

Charlene sees his appreciation for the beautiful house. It's what she doesn't see that intrigues her. "You knew where Woo Woo lived? Have you been here before?"

"Nope," says Terrell, dreading where this conversation could go. And there it goes.

"You checked Woo Woo out," Charlene says. She even points a finger at the detective. Woo Woo thinks, "Such a lovely man." That thought is about to be decimated.

"I checked you all out," says Terrell. "You were all cleared by the way."

"How do you know we're not involved?" says Lexie.

"I don't," says Terrell. "What I do know is that no one in the yoga class left the studio that morning, so you couldn't have stolen the watch. None of you have a criminal record so are unlikely to know a fence. You have no connection to Newhouse, and you are all financially stable."

"Some more stable than others apparently," says Lexie. Everyone laughs. Lexie is not sure it was a joke.

Kristi is on edge, but she appreciates the efforts her friends and the police detective are going to on her behalf. It's this awareness that stops her from ripping open the file folders Terrell has in his hand and diving headfirst into Charlene's briefcase. (A lovely red faux-alligator bag.) She agrees with everyone that they should have a quick bite first, then spread out the evidence. The lunch works. People stay deliberately away from the reason they're all enjoying one another's company and do just that – enjoy themselves. The elephant in the room recedes to a corner.

As Woo Woo and Lexie make coffee and chai tea, Terrell and Charlene clear the table and spread their papers out. Kristi tries not to gawk but it's like driving by the scene of an accident. You can't help your neck from swiveling. Once the team is seated around the table, Terrell turns to Kristi.

"Your business partner is an ass."

Now it's Kristi who doesn't know whether to cry or to laugh. She opts for door number 2. "I have discovered that very recently."

"Is he a dishonest ass?" Lexie wants to know, bringing everyone back to the matter at hand. Literally.

"My guess would be 'yes,' but we'll need Charlene to answer that," Terrell says. Charlene is already comparing the photos the detective took to her itemized list of purchases. She makes a number of Xs and check marks. Then the calculator comes out on her iPad. Woo Woo misses the days when calculators whirred.

Terrell has passed around the pics for everyone else to see while they wait for the auditor to announce her findings. That takes about 20 minutes. Terrell and Woo Woo make more tea.

Finally, Charlene looks up. "Thieving ass it is."

Kristi opts for door number one. Thieving ass is bad. How could she have misread this man for so long? How could she have believed he was a good man? How could she have wanted more from him than a monthly business meeting? Then Kristi's cries turn to laughter. Thieving ass is good. If she can threaten Jaxx with legal action, he just might back out of the business with little fight and no money. She turns to Charlene. "Tell me what you found?"

"There's little doubt some of the gym equipment Jaxx bought for Vitality+ is now calling his condo home. That will be worth thousands. It's equally clear other 'business' purchases – several pieces of art, a couch, and an espresso maker, at first glance – are nowhere near the business."

"How much are we talking?" Terrell asks. He senses the unasked question. "Theft over $5,000 is an indictable offence in Canada. Carries a maximum prison sentence of 10 years."

Kristi gasps. It had never occurred to her Jaxx could go to prison. She's not sure if she wants this. Worse, she's not sure she doesn't.

"The key is leverage," says Charlene bringing the group back to the reason they're all here. "Going to court will be expensive and time consuming. Kristi needs him gone now, with his tail between his legs and his wallet empty."

The question is how to do that. The question is also can Kristi afford to keep the business running without a partner. The answer to the first issue involves asking Terrell for another favor, and one that might be unethical. The detective has been dealing with criminals and their collateral damage for long enough to know where the women before him have gone in their minds, what they want, and why they're hesitating. He makes it easy for them.

"I can bring Jaxx into the station, lay out what we've found, and let him know what he's facing. I'll also make it clear Kristi does not want to lay charges." He turns to Kristi to confirm. She nods. "That should strike the fear of god into him and give him the out you want him to take."

"Then we can move in with an offer," says Charlene. "Give me three days. Paperwork will be ready. All Jaxx has to do is sign on the dotted line."

"Can I have the espresso maker?" Lexie asks.

Chapter 17.

Ariel puts her key in the lock and opens the door to Vitality+. It's grey and cloudy outside. A perfect match to her mood. This has not been a great month she admits to herself. She has been short-tempered with clients. And Nathan. Jaxx doesn't count. He's an ass. It's okay to get on his case. He doesn't usually come in on Sundays; in fact, he hasn't been around much the last week, and that's okay with Ariel. Being an ass and all.

Ariel opens the blinds and lets in whatever light can seep through the clouds. She turns the TVs on mute and starts dragging out some of the more portable props: weights, stability balls, resistance bands. She surveys her work and nods. Gym looks good. Ariel turns and walks to the staff lunchroom. She fills the coffeemaker (they really do need to invest in one from the 21st century) and breathes in the aroma of Walmart's dark roast. A hint of a smile hovers somewhere near her lips.

Sundays are unpredictable. They can be dead as a nit or overflowing with sweaty bodies trying to burn off a Saturday night hangover. Either way, it's only one person on duty per shift, and today that person is Ariel. She sips her coffee. It is good. Maybe the day won't be all that bad. Maybe no one will show up.

It takes less than 15 minutes for Ariel's optimism to vanish. At 7:15 Byron Newhouse and his son walk through the door. They wave and smile as they head for the changeroom. Ariel looks at Christian and waves back. The message is clear. She knows she needs to be polite to all the gym's clients, but she doesn't have it in her today to pretend she has any time for Byron Newhouse. Another ass.

She remembers the day, with some horror, that the harlot came in screaming at him. Until that day, Ariel did not know she knew the word harlot. Ariel was mortified at the scene – in her gym, her world. In hindsight, she should have seen this coming. Her mother would have. Her mother could spot a no-good guy from six blocks away. She was like a bloodhound sniffing out debauchery.

Ariel hasn't forgiven Newhouse for the upheaval. Not that he has asked for forgiveness. He assumes it is his right to control the room, even when that control is wrested from him by a woman scorned. Scorned, really? Now Ariel has to worry that she has more of her mother in her than she ever imagined.

There are no personal training sessions scheduled, so Ariel goes to the laundry room and brings out a hamper of towels for folding. That way she can watch the front door, staff the info desk, and not be totally bored out of her mind. Maybe she can figure out where she ever heard the word scorned. Or harlot.

Byron Newhouse is already on the hybrid. He's running the treadmill working up to full speed. The elliptical will be next Ariel knows. Christian is on the other side of the gym lifting weights. The resistance bands close at hand. These two have a routine. For dad, it's work as hard as you can as fast as you can and be sure everyone sees your pecs. For Christian, it's stay as far away from your father as possible.

Two more members have entered the gym. Ariel makes an effort to welcome them. Some comment about the weather. Her basket of towels now neatly folded, she picks up the hamper. One of the newcomers reaches over. "Let me take that for you."

Not everyone is an ass, Ariel reminds herself.

Newhouse is strutting to the changeroom, but no one is looking. What a waste, he thinks. Newhouse knows he looks good, and not just for a man his age, whatever that means. The developer spends time on his physique making sure muscles are defined, abs prominent, and shoulders broad. Unlike his father. The man never saw the inside of a gym; of course, he couldn't afford a gym. Newhouse offered to buy him a membership. The offer was rebuffed. "What do I need a stupid machine for. I can walk. I can do pushups."

But he never did. Dropped dead of a heart attack at 61 working in the small bakery he had owned and operated for more than 35 years. The bakery is gone; a bridal salon in its place. That's fitting, Newhouse thinks. He resents the fact his parents never swooned over his achievements. His father was indifferent at best, dismissive at worst. His mother would be proud, but she lived in her own world in a nursing home in downtown Halifax. Newhouse visited, as dutiful sons do, but his mother had long since left this sphere. The nurses, however, know how successful he is.

The developer waves to his son to let him know they'll be leaving soon. He sees Christian dutifully start to put away his equipment. Newhouse smiles at Ariel as he passes the info desk. She turns and leaves the room. Newhouse is getting a lot of that lately. But Newhouse isn't going to let the hired help get to him.

Still, he prefers to be the welcome centre of attention. He figures it's the damn watch. It's drawn a lot of interest and not all of it welcome by gym staff or members. Newhouse figures the animosity should die down soon. The case is basically dead. The cop called him a couple of days ago with a non-update update. There has been no progress finding the watch. Newhouse doubts there ever will be. Whoever stole that watch is long gone or they've hidden that watch somewhere so obscure no one will ever find it.

The big man couldn't be more wrong.

Once his dad enters the changeroom, Christian starts to leave the workout area. It's not that he doesn't love his father or want to spend time with him, but the truth is life is easier at a distance from Byron Newhouse. Christian has grappled with this reality his whole life.

He remembers his sixth birthday party. His dad went all out, decorations, games, bouncy castles (plural), and so much food. Mind you, six-year-olds would have preferred hot dogs to foie gras. (Christian's mom told everyone it was real dinosaur poop.) Christian remembers being so excited about his birthday. He had asked for the Tiger 2XL – his very own toy robot. It talked, it played games, it cracked jokes. Christian didn't get the Tiger Robot. He got a leather holster with a replica Derringer pistol. Engraved. Probably cost his dad a mint. Christian gave it to Bobby Whitcombe a week later. Apropos, Christian thinks. Whitcombe is doing six years in a federal penitentiary for armed robbery.

Christian hears the rush of water as soon as he steps inside the changeroom. His dad is in the shower and will have to fix his hair when he gets out. That gives Christian time to change and make a quick exit to the car. (He'll shower at home.) He leaves his dad a note and makes a hasty retreat. If Jade were here, they'd go for coffee. She's studying though and unavailable for the entire day. Christian decides he'll do the same. It's really time he finished his PhD. That would be something to celebrate. Christian knows how he'd like to celebrate becoming Dr. Newhouse. He'd like to get married. Of course, someone will have to resuscitate his father.

Ariel has fifteen minutes left on her shift. Turned out to be a quiet day after all. She starts to wipe down a few pieces of equipment. Members are supposed to do this. Yeah, right. She hears the phone ring and wonders if she can ignore it. She can't. A quick dash across the room and Ariel is saying, "Vitality+."

It's Jaxx. Probably just getting up. Or getting laid. Ariel doesn't care either way. "The cop is coming in tomorrow. Make sure the changeroom is so clean you can eat off the floor," Jaxx says and hangs up.

That fuckin' watch.

It's 6:30 in the morning. Still dark, but surprisingly mild for this time of year. Perhaps the sign of a good day to come. Terrell makes his way to his car. There will be very little traffic at this hour. He turns left onto the Bedford Highway. Ten minutes later he's pulling into the parking lot at

Vitality+. The lights are on, and a few bodies are visible in the large glass window that fronts the gym.

The detective makes sure he's ready for his morning.

Coffee. *Check.*

Danish. *Check.*

iPad. *Check.*

Waiting is second nature to Terrell. It's part of the fabric of life as a cop. You wait for forensics to report, you wait for witnesses to show up, you wait for suspects to misstep. Terrell is a patient man, but he comes prepared.

The detective sticks his head in the gym office. It's empty. Jaxx is probably keeping his distance. Can't blame him, Terrell thinks. His world has imploded and it's about to get worse. He gives Ariel a quick wave as he makes his way to the changeroom. Someone Terrell has never seen before is getting changed. Terrell nods and stakes out a spot on one of the long benches in front of the lockers. It gives him a clear view of the door but is far enough away from the showers he won't be moist within five minutes.

Terrell can feel the member's eyes on him. Nova Scotians are polite by nature, or at least upbringing. Terrell imagines Mr. X is trying to figure out if it would be rude to ask who the hell the strange man is sitting on the bench in his changeroom eating pastry. Terrell bets Mr. X will say nothing. Terrell wins. It won't always go this way. Someone, likely from Ontario, will ask him what he's doing, and he'll flash his shield. If pressed, he'll simply say, "Security."

As Mr. X exits the room, two other members walk in. Terrell has seen them before although he can't put names to the faces. For the next hour, there is a steady trickle of men in and out of the changeroom. Terrell keeps a record of when someone enters and how long they stay, even what they do. (Shower? No shower?) Three people ask him who he is and what he's doing. The shield gives them the answer they're looking for.

There are times when the changeroom is empty or there is someone in the shower and the locker area is vacant. Terrell times those opportunities. At no time does it exceed ninety seconds. Time enough for someone to open a locker and steal a watch. It would have to be a very confident someone though. Someone who has either done this before or has an easy excuse if caught. It's not looking good for Christian.

According to Terrell's watch it's almost 8 o'clock. He's ready to wrap up. Perhaps he'll join the yogis for a coffee. His is long gone. Terrell tosses his paper cup and pastry wrapper in the garbage can. He puts his iPad under his left arm and turns to exit. He misses running smack into Nathan by inches. The personal trainer is standing there with an armload of clean towels. It takes him a few seconds to close his gaping mouth. So Jaxx didn't tell all the staff he was coming. Terrell does what the gym owner should have. "Routine check."

Nathan gives him a weak smile and starts putting the towels in racks. He gathers up the dirty towels. Terrell isn't moving. Nathan, finished with his chores, heads for the door, arms loaded with damp terrycloth. He shoots Terrell a questioning glance, not sure what the immobile detective is doing. Terrell is thinking. Thinking how easy it would be to slip a watch inside a pile of dirty laundry.

* * *

The yoga participants are filing out the door. Today was a tough class. Each month Kristi picks an advanced pose for everyone to work toward. The goal for this month is bird of paradise, or Svarga Dvijasana. (Try saying that fast three times.) It is a one-legged standing pose that requires flexibility, balance, and strength. And naturally there's a bind. Everyone but Bhodi and Woo Woo lost their balance. Most of the class never even got one leg off the ground and in the air.

Lexie and Charlene are heading for the exit when Nathan comes out of the changeroom. He looks disconcerted. It's a look Lexie recognizes. He has sometimes given it to her. She starts to offer a smile but stops short. Close behind Nathan is Terrell.

What the hell is going on here? Lexie can feel her heart racing. Charlene looks up. Uncertain what is going on. But Lexie's fingers clenching her arm tell her something is very wrong.

They are all now at the café and Lexie isn't sure how to bring up the issue of Nathan and the changeroom. Woo Woo does it for her. There are seven of them nestled in the cozy corner Charlene has once again snagged. Lexie thinks it would be easier if the café simply put "Reserved" on the table. "We didn't expect to see you today?" Woo Woo says.

"Just checking out the changeroom," says Terrell. "It's a busy spot. Lots of company." He grins at Charlene and Lexie. Lexie can feel herself starting to relax.

For the next twenty minutes, the conversation bounces from inflation to the decaf coffee on sale at Costco to the breakdown of another celebrity marriage. Lexie swears she has never heard of these people. Bonnie and Honey get up to leave. Lexie and Charlene are right behind them clearing up their coffee cups and plates. Kristi checks her watch and stands up to go. Before she can leave, Terrell asks if he can have a minute of her time. He feels the tension level rise. Charlene feels Lexie's fingers back on her arm.

Terrell would rather speak to Kristi in private. Kristi makes it clear anything he says to her, she'll only repeat to her friends.

"I need the employment files for all your employees. Background check."

"Didn't you do that already?" Charlene wants to know.

"I spoke to everyone who was at the gym that morning," Terrell says, "but we didn't need the employment files."

"Until now," says Charlene. She can feel her arm go numb with pain.

Daily Thoughts – Woo Woo
Monday, October 21st

I have a lot to share. Most of it is a little distressing.

Lexie did not have a good day, and I'm not sure why. I'd like to help her, but it's hard to help when you don't know what the problem is. It's got something to do with Nathan. He's one of the wonderful trainers at Vitality+. I mean he seems wonderful. In hindsight, I've probably never said more than ten words to him, but Lexie is enamored. Well, not enamored. There is something there though. (No, it's not that. Of that, I'm sure.)

Michael was doing a stakeout today at the gym, in the changeroom. When he came out (so Charlene tells me), Nathan was white as a sheet. Lexie was too. Charlene said she nearly broke her arm. Again, not sure why. What is it with this guy that has Lexie in knots? I could ask her, but something tells me that might be a step too far too soon in our friendship.

It got worse if you can believe it. Michael asked Kristi for the employment records. Seems simple enough. The police are doing a deeper dive, that's what Michael says. Charlene isn't buying it. She says bank account information is part of employment records. If a company hands them over (and Kristi did!), no privacy laws are broken because employees have no expectation of privacy with respect to their employment files. This means the police can access bank accounts.

Why is the question. What does that tell them? I know, I know. If someone sold the watch and deposited the money in their account, it would be a red flag. Really, someone has eluded the police for three weeks but they're sloppy enough to put a whopping big sum of money in their personal bank account. I'd put it in the freezer. (I have a lovely freezer, a Hestan. It has an orange door!)

Anyway, you understand what I'm saying. I tried to tell Lexie this, but the reassurance is premised on the fact that Nathan is a thief. And we're back to Lexie being distressed. Charlene says she has to get a grip. Maybe I'll invite everyone over for dinner. I have some Cornish hens in the Hestan. They'd be delicious. Maybe comfort food would be better. A seafood chowder, perhaps. With lobster. (I must ask if anyone is allergic to shellfish.)

We did bird of paradise today. It's not an easy pose – Kristi says it's an advanced pose – and I did so well. Better than Bhodi. I saw him put his leg down before I did, and he knows it. I'm not supposed to care. Yoga teaches us it's not about competition, it's about our own journey. Still, Bhodi is an ass. It feels good to get one over on him. And now I feel bad for feeling good.

Charlene, Lexie, and I have decided to meet before class for a cup of tea and a muffin. It's not like this will become a regular thing, but it's a way to check in with Lexie. She knows this, and she didn't object.

I really do think we are friends.

Sincerely,

Shonda Aeron

PS Perhaps Michael would like to join us for chowder.

Chapter 18.

There is ketchup on the table, the napkin dispenser, Terrell's blue checked shirt, Terrell's forehead. There is no ketchup on Terrell's breakfast plate and no ketchup anywhere remotely near his boss, who is bowled over in a fit of laughter. "Ha ha," says Terrell as he heads for the washroom. No one else in the diner is laughing. His SIG Sauer P226 is visible on his hip.

Despite the condiment fiasco, Terrell enjoys his monthly breakfast meetings with Inspector Jennifer Boone. Purportedly for business, it's an opportunity for two law enforcement veterans to get away from the station and the pressure for a few minutes and have some bacon and eggs. They talk business; it is, after all what connects them indelibly, but the conversation is not about finding solutions or reporting in. It is about conversing.

There's a Tide To Go stain remover stick in the bathroom. Clearly, Terrell is not the first casualty of a faulty ketchup dispenser. Thing actually works. Spots be gone. Terrell decides he really needs to get a life. I mean, when stain remover is a highlight of your day. He makes his way back to the table. Boone is wiping tears off her face between bites of hashbrown.

"Lookin' good," she says and bowls over again.

"I'm going to change the subject," says Terrell, forking eggs and English muffin into his mouth. "How does theft sound. I have a suspect and a non-suspect?"

"Who are they?" Boone wants to know. She's sitting a little straighter. This is a development.

"They're one and the same," says Terrell. "Nathan Young."

"I'll need a little more."

"I've been looking at who could get into the changeroom and out in time. I haven't been looking at who could hang around for an opportune moment."

"And Young could?"

Terrell explains about stocking the changeroom. A personal trainer or other employee standing there with a stack of towels would not look suspicious, and he could take his time fussing with the dirty laundry and replacing the towel racks.

"Sounds promising."

"Could be," Terrell agrees. "Here's the bad news. We don't have motive, and we don't have a money trail. I checked. Taylor's clean. So is everyone else as far as their bank records go."

"So this isn't about money. It's got to be personal."

Terrell is almost through his eggs benny when his phone rings. It's Woo Woo. Boone looks down at the phone and up at Terrell. "Since when do you put the name of a witness in your contacts?"

* * *

The studio is starting to fill up. People are saying hello to one another, getting their props in order, warming up. There's a debate about whether Kristi will make them do bird of paradise again today. Kristi stays silent, and shrugs knowingly. Bhodi looks at Woo Woo. "Bring it," she says to herself. Perhaps a little more meditation wouldn't hurt.

Archina is the last to arrive. She's running a little late and hurries into the storage area to grab a mat. She brings it into the studio maneuvering around the plastic buddha, Honey in downward dog, and Bhodi in some contortion Woo Woo doubts is even yoga.

Archina unrolls her mat. And screams.

Everyone rushes over to see what's wrong. Sitting like a little lotus in a vinyl sea of pink foam is a man's watch. A very expensive watch they have all seen pictures of. Kristi bends down to retrieve the watch. Honey stops her mid-bend. "Don't touch anything. We need to phone Detective

188

Terrell." Woo Woo is already dialing. Charlene is also on her phone. She's busy taking pictures.

* * *

"Gotta go," Terrell says, standing up and reaching for his wallet.

"What's up?" Boone asks, also rising.

"Don't know. But they don't tell me to come right away unless it's important."

Boone would like to say, "Really, you know 'them' that well, do you?" Instead, she says, "I'll go with you."

Terrell shoots her a look. "Since when do you accompany detectives to a scene?"

Boone heads for the door. Over her shoulder she says, "Since they started putting a witness's name in their contacts."

It takes the two officers about 20 minutes to get to the studio. When they walk in, 10 men and women are in plank moving into upward dog. Kristi tells everyone to move into child's pose. She looks at Terrell and points to an area in the studio blocked on three sides by bolsters. "There's something you need to see."

Everyone comes out of child's pose, two of them gracefully. They make their way to the cordoned area and hover. Honey steps forward. "This fell out of the mat when Archina unrolled it this morning."

"Son of a bitch," says Boone. She feels ten sets of eyes on her. "Inspector Jennifer Boone. His boss." She jerks a thumb in Terrell's direction and tries not to grin. This really isn't a grinning situation. Not now, anyway. In a month, when she tells this in the lunchroom, it will be hilarious.

"We assumed you wouldn't want us to leave," Honey says looking straight at Terrell. "That's why we decided we might as well do a little yoga until you got here."

Message received, Boone thinks. I know where your loyalty lies. She makes a mental note to put this in Terrell's performance review. In the back of her mind, she thinks this woman who has taken control of the room looks familiar. Boone makes it a point of remembering faces. An asset in her line of work. This face eludes her. For now.

Terrell has put on a pair of black nitrile gloves and is placing the watch in an evidence bag. He holds up a hand to quell the questions that are starting to erupt. "We'll need to speak with each of you individually. That's going to take a little time. Go grab yourselves a coffee, finish class, take a shower. Just don't leave."

A quiet voice behind him says, "Before you speak with anyone, you really should have a coffee with us."

So this is Woo Woo, Boone thinks. Then she looks at Terrell. So, not Woo Woo.

Terrell hesitates for a split second. "No one leave. Come on Charlene. Let's get a coffee." Charlene starts for the door. Boone comes up behind her. Two women come on either side of her. Lexie introduces herself. Woo Woo holds out her hand. "I'm Woo Woo."

The corner table and chairs are taken when the crew arrives. By the time they have a cup of coffee three minutes later, Charlene has the coveted seating area covered in napkins, stir sticks and sugar packets. "Thought this would give us a bit more privacy." Boone thinks she's going to put Charlene's name in her contact list.

"What's up?" Terrell asks. There's no impatience in his tone. He knows these women, and he knows how to get the most information out of people. Pushy rarely wins the race.

"The watch isn't Newhouse's," Charlene says. Boone is definitely going to put this woman's contact in her phone.

Terrell waits. It's impressive to watch his technique, Boone thinks. It's been a while. She should get out of the office more.

"Newhouse's watch is a Nautilus 7010. This is a 7011." Now Charlene waits. Terrell is thinking this through. He's not doubting Charlene; he's running the implications through his mind.

Boone does not have either of their patience. "How do you know?" She can feel the disapproval. This is not how things are done.

"I downloaded pictures of the original watch when it first went missing. When this one unfurled this morning, something wasn't quite right." She pushes her phone over to Boone and Terrell. Lexie pushes her phone over as well. "The 7010," Lexie says pointing to her phone. "The 7011," Lexie says pointing to Charlene's phone.

Terrell and Boone spend several minutes looking at the two images. There are undoubtedly variations once you look carefully. The shape of the watches is slightly different, the font of the date, and the beveling of the numbers.

"We have no doubt you'd figure this out," Woo Woo says to Terrell. She shoots Boone a look. "We thought we'd save you some time."

"We also thought that if Newhouse says the watch is his – and he might for a whole bunch of reasons – there'd be no need to look closely at this watch. You might just take him at his word. Case solved," Lexie says.

Boone never wants to cross these women.

Terrell and his boss spend the rest of the morning interviewing the yogis and hearing – consistently – about the magical appearance of the rose gold watch. They agree to interview witnesses separately to save on time and effort, and on the unspoken understanding that it is highly unlikely any of these people had anything to do with the original theft. There is one exception to the interview plan: Archina. Terrell and Boone interview her together and they interview her first. Again, not out of suspicion of her guilt but to ensure they get as complete a summary of events as they could.

Archina told them she was running late. She'd stopped for gas. (There was a receipt.) At the studio, she grabbed a mat from the cotton rope basket in the entry way and went directly into the practice area. Kristi was calling everyone together. Terrell asks how she held the mat. The question obviously confuses Archina. Boone tries to explain. In the end, they learn Archina had not placed the rolled mat under her arm; she'd grabbed it at the top and carried it in like a large jug of water with a handle.

Terrell and Boone nod at each other. This means the watch was well buried inside the yoga mat. If someone had shoved it in at the last minute, it would have fallen out the bottom of the mat or Archina would have seen the watch when she grabbed the top. Terrell thanks Archina and tells her she has been very helpful. He doesn't tell her they believe she is innocent, but the implication is clear: a friendly smile, a warm tone, and a collegial pat on the shoulder.

Before Terrell can draw up a list for the next round of interviews, Boone says, "I'll do Woo Woo," and she's out the door. About as subtle as a June bug on a hairy leg.

Terrell opts for Lexie next. She's observant. She's not reluctant to speak her mind. She's got nothing to do with this incident. Lexie confirms Archina's story. She saw Archina dash in through the studio door, grab a mat, and quietly claim a spot at the back of the room. Then she screams. It gets a little confusing after that. Everyone runs over to see what's wrong. Lexie is at the outer edges of the group. She can't see the mat, but she can hear, "Oh, my God!" Is that....?" "Where did it come from?" Then she hears Honey tell everyone to step back and not touch anything. She tells Woo Woo to call "Detective Terrell," but Woo Woo is already on the phone. (Lexie gives Terrell a big grin.) So is Charlene, although at that point Lexie isn't sure why.

Lexie also goes out of her way to make it clear she doesn't think for one moment that Archina put that watch in the mat or took the original watch. Terrell doesn't say anything. His silence is telling.

"Who do you think did it?" Lexie asks.

"You know I can't tell you that."

"How about I say a name and if you think it's that person you blink twice?"

"I'm not playing," says Terrell, but he realizes this is not a game for Lexie.

Lexie is waiting for Charlene. They're meeting Woo Woo at the café. Lexie is pacing back and forth across the entranceway to the gym. She's trying to look nonchalant. She's failing. Nathan (she's calling him that now) is behind the front desk. He waves at her and smiles. She waves back and hopes the look on her face resembles a smile.

Since she saw Nathan and Terrell exit the men's changeroom yesterday, Lexie has been fretting. Something is not right. She can feel it. She also saw it – whatever 'it' is – on Nathan's face. Lexie is getting nothing out of Terrell. She's tried being subtle (well, subtle for Lexie). She's tried being blunt. Man, that police training must be something else. Terrell didn't move a microfiber. But something is up.

There's nothing for it but to grab the bull by the horns Lexie has decided. Nathan is the bull. Still, who willingly confronts a bull if you're not in Spain? Lexie continues to pace. And count. She's given herself thirty seconds. At second twenty-five, she strides to the front desk.

* * *

The shouting starts at 10:25. Terrell knows because he checks his watch as soon as he hears the angry yelling. The detective is midway through an interview with Bhodi (which seems to be more about Bhodi than what happened earlier this morning). Terrell gets up quickly and makes his way to the studio door. Byron Newhouse is trying to roughhouse his way inside. He's not getting past Boone.

"Mr. Newhouse, I presume," Boone says.

195

"Who the hell are you?" Newhouse demands.

"Inspector Boone. Jennifer Boone. You can call me Inspector."

The rank takes some of the wind out of Newhouse's huffing and puffing. He scans the crowd that has now gathered around him. "You found my watch," he says looking at Terrell, someone he recognizes and maybe someone he can even bully.

"Mr. Newhouse, why don't you come inside. I was just about to call you. Inspector Boone and I need to speak with you." Terrell ushers him inside, almost like rolling out a welcoming mat.

Newhouse straightens and walks into the office where Terrell has been interviewing the yogis. (Boone took the lunchroom.) He swaggers just a bit, like he's won the first three rounds of a bantamweight match. Terrell can't help but smile. As he turns to walk into the room, he glances at the front desk. Nathan is standing there frozen. Terrell stops suddenly to see what has so upset the personal trainer. To his surprise, the answer is Lexie.

Chapter 19.

Byron Newhouse was in the middle of berating his construction foreman when his assistant interrupted. Trina knows not to interrupt mid-tirade. Newhouse was about to let lose on Trina when she whispered something in his ear. Newhouse grabbed his car keys and his coat. He told the foreman to get out. He forgot to thank Trina.

Newhouse called Christian from the car. "How do you know my watch has been found?" He forgot to say good morning to his son.

"Jade called me."

"How the hell does your girlfriend know my watch has been found?"

"Ariel called her."

This shut Newhouse up. Why the hell would Ariel call Jade? So Jade would call Christian? Why not call Christian herself? Oh dammit. Ariel isn't friends with the gold digger is she? You know what, Newhouse no longer cares. Let these women do what they will. He's getting his watch back. Christian is in the clear.

Newhouse smirked. Things were going his way. As they should. He hung up on his son.

Newhouse is not smirking now. He's annoyed. He's puzzled, and there is a trickle of fear inching its way vertebrae by vertebrae up his back. Newhouse has decided he doesn't like the police inspector. This may be his month for irritating women – and he's only known this one for six minutes.

They're sitting in the gym office. Boone on one side of the table, Terrell on the other side with him. They've found his watch. They show him an evidence bag. His watch is inside. They ask him if it's his watch. Newhouse looks at them like they have ten heads. "Of course, it's my watch. Who else's watch would it be?"

Terrell pushes the evidence bag closer. "Take your time."

Newhouse sighs. It will be a month of irritating women and idiots. He picks up the bag. He looks at the watch. Nice watch. He congratulates himself on his good taste. He senses the cops watching him closely. He peers at the watch thinking about how much more impressive it will be on his wrist than the Omega. He wishes his father were here to see him now.

"Yep. That's my watch."

"No, it isn't," says Boone quietly. Ominously. A vertebrae twitches on Newhouse's back.

"What the hell are you talking about? It's my watch. Do you think anybody else in this place can afford a Patek Philippe."

"Yes," says Boone softly. Worryingly. (She had a great talk with Woo Woo.)

Newhouse is taken aback – for a split second. There's no one in this pissant gym who has as much money as he does. "It's my watch."

"Your watch is a Nautilus 7010," Terrell says.

Newhouse doesn't wait for any more drivel. Time to show these people who's boss. "I know my own goddamn watch."

"This is a Nautilus 7011," Terrell says. He can't help adding, "It's more expensive than the Nautilus 7010."

Newhouse is furious. He has been humiliated. Byron Newhouse does not do humiliation. He inflicts humiliation.

In the car driving back to the office, he replays the interview with the cops. He replays the whole episode from his arrival. Marching in. Demanding to speak with whoever is in charge. Accusing the detective and the sergeant, or whatever the hell she is, of withholding information. Threatening to sic his lawyer on the entire police force.

Then seeing the watch. His watch. Newhouse can't believe it's not his watch. Looks exactly the same to him, but he doesn't think the cops are lying. He's no conspiracy theorist. That means someone put a watch that resembles his very closely in a yoga mat where it would most certainly be found.

Who the hell would do that Newhouse wonders. The only reason he can fathom is to put an end to the investigation. To make it look like the missing watch has been found, no insurance claim, no criminal charges. Life as usual.

Oh Christian, what have you done?

"Oh God, that was fun." Boone can't help smiling. She's almost giddy.

"You really have to get out more," Terrell says.

Boone gives him a small sneer that turns into a giggle. Good grief. "I particularly enjoyed speaking with Mr. Newhouse. Man can't even recognize his own watch. Or can he." She looks at Terrell.

He understands the questions she's asking. "Man isn't stupid, just arrogant. Assumed the watch was his. I probably would have too."

"Do you think he had something to do with this?"

It's the $60,000 question. (According to Charlene's research, it may be the $160,000 question.) "I can't fathom who would do this," Terrell says. "The why is easy."

"You think they want us off the case."

"Can't think of any other reason why someone would plant a watch that mirrors the missing watch."

"They think we're getting close."

Terrell agrees. The question though is close to whom? There isn't a leading suspect in the case. Truth be told, there really isn't even a strong contender. But it looks like someone thinks there is. "This was protection. End the investigation. Keep your loved one safe."

"Makes sense," Boone agrees. "But who the hell has $60,000 to throw away on a watch they are never going to wear?"

They both know Woo Woo does. They also both know that on a list of one hundred suspects Woo Woo is 101. She just doesn't have motive or opportunity, at least for the theft. Anyone, it appears, could have jammed the watch inside the yoga mat. Kristi told them the studio is not locked. Indeed, when classes are not under way, members are welcome to go to the studio to meditate, do some yoga or pilates, and unwind.

No record is kept of who goes into the studio when it's empty although Kristi thinks it's rarely used outside classes. Terrell could ask Jaxx, but he hasn't been in very much over the past few days Kristi said. Terrell knows his absence has nothing to do with the watch.

"You said Newhouse and the girlfriend both thought the thief was Christian. Could he have put the watch in the mat?"

Terrell shrugs. "Sure. Any gym member could have put the watch in the mat, and Christian might have access to the funds for a new watch. But why? There's not a chance in hell that kid would defy his father enough to steal his watch in the first place?"

"Even if it was for his girlfriend?"

"Maybe," Terrell concedes. "I'll ask him to meet us at the station this afternoon. If nothing else, that will scare the crap out of him."

"And his father," Boone points out. "Newhouse himself could be the culprit if he thinks his son is in danger."

"Just can't see Newhouse throwing away sixty grand. He likes to flash his money around."

"What about the girlfriend?"

"Lives like a poor church mouse, but I didn't do a deep dive on her finances or any of the gym members outside Newhouse. No need. We were looking for someone who needed money, not someone who had money to burn."

Christian has heard all about the mysterious appearance of a Patek Philippe in a yoga mat. His father has gone on at great length. To be honest, Christian could care less about the newfound watch. He's not sure why it's bothering his father so much. He called to bark at his son after he left the gym, then again when he got to the office. Christian didn't answer the third call.

If anyone knows how Byron Newhouse thinks, it's his son. Christian knows after the first call that his father has embarrassed himself in front of the police and the gym members. He likely yelled and thumped his chest. Let everyone know he's the big man on campus. Then he couldn't even identify his own watch. Christian is embarrassed for him.

It's the second call that has Christian puzzled. His father is pushing for something, but what. No doubt his dad would have liked to claim the 7011 arm candy. It would have ended this whole mess with the police, and it would have given him a more expensive watch (even if he didn't know it). That's not happening. His father isn't usually one to cling to the past. He barrels ahead. That means he's holding on for a reason. Christian heads to the small kitchen on the fourth floor of the Faculty of Management building. He pours himself a mug of hot water from the Keurig and dunks a green teabag into the cup.

The water turns a murky sage then deepens to the color of sea green. Christian continues dipping the bag in and out of the hot water. *Son of a bitch.* His father thinks he put the watch in the yoga mat.

Christian's reverie is interrupted by the ringing of his phone. He's in no mood to speak with his father. He lifts his finger to dismiss the call. It's not his father. It's the police.

Daily Thoughts – Lexie
Tuesday, October 22nd

Spoke to Nathan today. Opened my mouth and words came out. I will never learn.

I thought I was being helpful. I was just being intrusive – and I have no right to intrude in his life. I had worked myself into a tizzy ever since I saw Nathan and Terrell coming out of the changeroom. It was the look on Nathan's face. And the look on Terrell's face. I knew Terrell suspected Nathan. Well, I thought I knew. Now, I've scared the hell out of Nathan, and I'm probably wrong.

Worked up the nerve to talk to Nathan about the changeroom incident, or non-incident as it may well turn out. Decided I would offer to pay for a lawyer if he needed one. I mean, what casual acquaintance you wave to three or four times a week wouldn't do the same thing? Steeled my nerves, strode to the front desk, opened my mouth. Three strikes.

Nathan was horrified. I could see it on his face. I'm not sure if he was horrified by my offer or my assertion that he was a suspect.

Stupid. Stupid. Stupid.

I embarrassed him. I embarrassed myself. Now he thinks I'm a loon. He'll want to stay away from me (like we were ever close). I don't know why I can't filter things around him. I'm a stand-up comedian for God's sake. I put down hecklers on a regular basis. I pivot to a different bit when I'm losing the audience. But no, when it comes to Nathan I can't seem to think clearly or speak like a regular human. The end result: he hates me. That was not what I was going for.

Oh yeah, some dipstick put a $60,000 watch in a yoga mat. Must have thought this would put an end to the police investigation. Clearly has not met Charlene. Now we have a real mystery. First, who has $60,000(ish). Second, who throws it away on Byron Newhouse. He showed up at the gym frothing at the mouth. Seemed to calm down after he discovered the watch he said was his wasn't his at all. (Boone told Woo Woo. I think she's fond of Woo Woo, but she just met her. I am so freakin' confused.)

I don't want to go to yoga tomorrow. I don't ever want to go back to the studio. I know I have to. I have to pretend its life as usual. I long for life as usual. Life before Nathan. I really am going to have to deal with this even if that means letting go. Totally. Permanently.

But like the Dixie Chicks I'm not ready to back down yet. I think I need some advice. Maybe I'll ask Woo Woo and Charlene.

I know who I won't be asking. Nathan.

Stupid. Stupid. Stupid.

LH

Chapter 20.

Terrell is wading through a tangle of paper. The forensic team has done a deep dive on the finances for each of the likely suspects in the Newhouse case. Previously, Terrell accessed their bank accounts and income tax files, but that doesn't tell how much money someone has in total or whether they have rich relatives. It wasn't important until now, until someone decided to tuck a watch worth, wait for it, $89,184 inside a yoga mat. This is the first time in Terrell's career he's had to look for someone who's throwing money away instead of stealing it for themselves.

The mound of paper is a little misleading. Terrell may have to read it all at some point, but, at the moment, there is one file on top that commands his attention. The forensic team flagged it. They're rarely wrong. If they're right, Christian Newhouse is in for a shock – and so is his father.

* * *

It's time to move forward. Kristi knows this, she just doesn't know what forward looks like. Usually when life is at an impasse, Kristi heads into the studio. She unwinds, stretches, flows, and finds balance there through yoga, meditation, and the calm that only a sanctuary can offer. Lately though when life is at an impasse, Kristi has been stepping outside the studio and meeting with her new friends.

Either way, it's time.

Charlene has an idea. She needs to see if the idea has legs. Perhaps the girls would like to come to dinner. Charlene opens her laptop to see what the Italian Market has to offer for a light supper.

Nathan feels bad for Lexie. He thinks she was trying to help. But, frankly, she just scared the bejeezus out of him. First, she offers him money for a lawyer. I mean she doesn't even know him, and she offers him money. What's that all about? Second, why would he need a lawyer? Unless he is in trouble. Unless he is going to be charged for stealing that watch.

Nathan has no idea what to do. He wonders if Lexie might.

Woo Woo has a funny feeling. She's had it all morning. It just won't go away. Woo Woo realizes it's not going to go away until she does something. Woo Woo sends a text.

The oatmeal raisin cookies are cooling on the rack beside the morning glory muffins. A pot of coffee is brewing and there is hot water for tea. There is even a pitcher of cranberry pomegranate juice. The doorbell rings. Charlene and Lexie are the first to arrive. A few minutes later Kristi walks through the front door. At exactly 2pm, Terrell rings the doorbell.

Everybody settles in, selects a beverage and a treat, or two. There is polite chitchat. It's Charlene who climbs atop the elephant in the room. "Woo Woo, this is lovely. Why the hell are we here?"

"I don't know," Woo Woo admits. "But something's wrong."

Terrell doesn't know whether to be horrified or impressed. "I think things are coming to a head on the case. Not that I can say much more."

Kristi breathes a sigh of relief. Charlene nods yes. Lexie turns a paler shade of white. "You might as well ask him," Woo Woo says.

Lexie has no idea how Woo Woo knows what Woo Woo appears to know, but Lexie is at her wits end. She feels like a fool for her behavior, which really can't be explained. It's not like she knows Nathan or anything about his life. What she does know is this: she's worried sick. "Are you going to arrest Nathan?"

Terrell looks at Lexie. It's a question he's not supposed to answer. It's a question he shouldn't answer while an investigation is ongoing and maybe even afterwards. But Woo Woo is right. Something is wrong here. Lexie is tense. She has circles under her eyes. Her skin is sallow. Her breathing shallow.

Whatever the hell is going on it's eating at her.

As a senior detective, Terrell has both experience and leeway. This investigation is his to run and that includes what he chooses to disclose and to whom. "No, Nathan is not going to be arrested. Nathan is not a suspect. For either stealing a watch or hiding one."

Lexie looks at Terrell. She was so sure he was going to arrest Nathan, at the very least had him at the top of his suspect list. She saw the look he had on his face when he left the changeroom. She saw the look on Nathan's face. Lexie turns to Charlene, to Woo Woo, to Kristi. No one seems surprised by Terrell's statement.

Lexie breaks into tears.

It takes several minutes and a new pot of tea, lemon ginger, to calm Lexie down. She feels she should be embarrassed. Sobbing is not something she does. Sobbing is not something feminists do. But Lexie does not feel embarrassed. She feels relieved. She feels safe.

Woo Woo can read a room. She reads this one. "Who's next?"

Charlene raises her hand. "I want to talk to you and Lexie. I have an idea. Its half formed. Perhaps by dinner tomorrow it will be more fully formed. My place. 6pm. Cannelloni."

Two down. One to go. As if by some unseen signal, the group turns to Kristi. Kristi sighs. "I need to tell Jaxx he's out. I need to make sure he'll go without a fight. I need to make sure he'll go without demanding money. I'm not sure how to do any of that."

"I can't help you with much of that," says Terrell, "but there is one thing I can do. I can reach out to Jaxx before you meet to let him know that no decision has been made about charging him with embezzlement. It's a big word that scares most people."

"Won't the timing make him suspicious?" Charlene asks.

"So what," Lexie says. The feminist is back. "As long as he walks away."

It's decided Kristi will call Jaxx later tonight and arrange a meeting for tomorrow morning. The less time he has to plot, the better. If he avoids her calls or refuses to meet, Kristi will threaten legal action of her own. Terrell will call Jaxx as soon as he gets back to the police station. The triad will linger at the café after yoga tomorrow in case Kristi needs any help. Or resuscitation.

Chapter 21.

Jaxx has stopped automatically answering his phone. He looks to see who's calling first and if he knows them. In particular, he's not taking any calls from Kristi. When he hears his phone ring, he reaches for his reading glasses. He's doing that now. Halifax Police Department. Dammit. Numb nuts is back.

Numb nuts sounds quite jovial. Just checking in. Only needs a minute of his time. So far, all Jaxx has done is grunt. "I wanted to update you. No official decision has been made with respect to laying fraud charges. If and when that changes, I will let you know."

Jaxx grunts. Terrell hangs up. One of them is grinning.

The detective has asked Newhouse, Christian, and Jade to come to the station. End of day is best. People are tired, they've had time to fret, their reflexes are slower. Jade and Christian arrive together, on time. Newhouse barrels in about five minutes later all bluster and big feeling.

Constable Reynolds meets the three of them in the front entranceway and signs them into the station. Newhouse demands to know what's going on. Constable Reynolds ignores him. He's bigger and better trained. He could squash this man like a bug.

Terrell is waiting for Jade. She appears calm and composed. He offers a seat and takes the one beside her. Very polite for an interrogation room.

"So, you know," Jade says.

"I do."

"That didn't take long."

"Well, honestly, it's not that big a secret. All someone had to do was look."

"But no one did," Jade points out. "Until now."

"Until now, no one had a reason to look."

Jade considers this. "I would have thought Byron would have checked."

"Point taken," says Terrell, "but Mr. Newhouse doesn't strike me as a man who looks beyond the surface."

"I have a great surface."

Terrell laughs. "Now it's broken. How do you want to do this?"

"It's nice of you to ask. I must admit I didn't expect that." Jade falls silent. Thinking. "I'm going to let you tell Byron. I'll tell Christian."

Terrell agrees. He stands up. "I'll have Christian brought in."

"I'm assuming I'm not in any legal trouble."

"I'm assuming you knew that when you put the watch in the yoga mat."

"I did, but sometimes the police don't play by the rules." Jade hesitates, "Do you think Christian stole his father's watch?

"I don't," Terrell says, "but it's not going to take him long to figure out you did."

* * *

Newhouse is frothing at the bit. He's been kept waiting unnecessarily. He's an important man. He has places to be. Yada yada yada. Constable Reynolds is in the viewing room enjoying a donair. Sauce is everywhere – on the plate, the desktop, the window – but not a drop on him. He jerks his head at Newhouse and grins. This is the highlight of his day.

Newhouse stops mid-rant when Terrell enters the room. Terrell ignores the questions and the accusations. "Tell me about your daughter-in-law to be."

The developer is almost apoplectic by this point. "She's a two-bit tart who's looking for a cash cow. That would be my idiot son. And my idiot son will not be marrying the tart."

Terrell can hear Constable Reynolds wailing with laughter in his ear bud. The detective has to admit he's enjoying this himself. "Ms. Dhillon has authorized me to share some information with you about the investigation."

"I knew it," Newhouse hisses. "Bitch stole my watch."

213

Terrell imagines Constable Reynolds is on the floor by now. "No, sir. Ms. Dhillon did not steal your watch. However, she did put the Nautilus 7011 in the yoga mat."

"Don't be absurd. She doesn't have that kind of money. I want to speak to your supervisor."

Terrell reminds him who his supervisor is. That takes the wind out of Newhouse's sails for a few seconds. "Apparently you have not met Ms. Dhillon's parents."

"What are you talking about?" Newhouse says, not nicely. "Why would I ever want to meet those people."

"Dhillon is Jade's mother's name. Her father's name is Dani. Kiann Dani."

"Don't be so stupid," Newhouse says dismissing Terrell with a flick of his hand. "Kiann Dani is a billionaire. Made his money in metals."

Terrell waits. This usually takes a few minutes. First comes denial.

"Oh my God, she told you her father was rich – and you believed her. How gullible can you be."

Terrell waits. Second comes anger. "That bitch. She kept this from us. Thought *we* weren't good enough for *her*."

"Perhaps she wanted to be sure you liked her more for her than her money." God, Terrell loves this job.

Here it is. Stage three. Negotiation. "I'll speak with her. Explain I was protecting

Christian from hurt. Explain I can be brusque, but I don't mean it."

"Good luck," says Terrell, "and I mean it."

* * *

It's almost 10pm. Kristi has been delaying this for as long as she can. She calls Jaxx. It goes to voice mail. She calls back. It goes to voice mail. Kristi can feel the knot in her stomach unravelling, her jaw unclenching, her headache retreating.

Sonofabitch.

There it is. What her mind, body, spirit has been waiting for. Kristi, at last, is pissed. Man stole from her – and not just stuff. Livelihood. Dignity.

Kristi calls Jaxx. He answers on the fourth ring. "I'm busy."

"I don't give a shit. I have you hands down for fraud, theft, and according to the cops, embezzlement. We're going to resolve this tomorrow once and for all – or I'm pressing charges. 8:30 tomorrow. The office."

Sonofabitch.

* * *

Madoff is frustrated. It's 9:45 pm. He should be in bed. Charlene should be in bed

215

with him. She would be reading. He would be snoring. Instead, they are here in front of the computer reading emails. Again.

The emails are unsettling. Madoff knows that. He also knows it has something to do with DNA. He saw the letters on the screen. He's heard Mama C. talking to Dora about this. He's seen her face when those letters are spoken.

Madoff doesn't like DNA.

* * *

Terrell has created a to-do list. Most of the items on it have nothing to do with Byron Newhouse and the case of the missing watch. That investigation has stalled. There is something hovering at the back of Terrell's mind. He knows that feeling well. It means the information he is looking for he already knows; he just hasn't put it all together. The only option: distraction. Hence the to-do list.

Most of the items have to do with other cases, cases like the Nautilus 7010 (and 7011) that are consuming more time than Terrell would like. But police work is a process. He's working the process. There are a few items on the list that don't have to do with a watch, or a theft, or a homicide. At the moment, the detective is heading through the front doors of Vitality+ with an essential oil gift box. Terrell isn't really sure what essential oils are but he saw some at Woo Woo's house yesterday, and he wanted to buy her a small thank you gift for all her help and thoughtfulness. He also wanted an excuse for heading back to the gym. There is something right in front of him. He just can't see it. At least that's what Terrell is telling himself.

The yoga class is still in session, as expected. The gift gives Terrell a reason for his presence; the timing gives him an opportunity to loiter. Perhaps inspiration will strike. The door to the office is open. Terrell can see Jaxx inside scrolling on his phone. He wonders for a second why the owner isn't on his computer as usual. He answers his own question: they've locked Jaxx out. Smart move.

Nathan is behind the front desk smiling at members as they walk in and out of the gym. He has a friendly word for everyone. Terrell doesn't believe its forced or fake. He makes his way toward the personal trainer. "No clients this morning?"

"I just finished a session." Nathan is not sure whether to be nervous or flattered.

"With Newhouse?"

"No, Mr. Newhouse isn't coming in as much lately. I imagine the watch thing has him upset." Nathan wonders if he's said too much.

Terrell thinks he's said just enough. "When did he start spending less time in the gym?"

Nathan may be Mr. Nice Guy, but he's not Mr. Stupid Guy. The causal chitchat is over, the detective is back. Nathan considers his answer. "Around the time the girlfriend came in and made a scene. Can't blame him for staying away. That really was embarrassing. She had everyone in the gym staring at her and Mr. Newhouse."

The yoga studio is emptying. Terrell turns toward the group. Nathan glances in the same direction. Lexie and Woo Woo are the first out the door. Woo Woo looks up. She smiles at Terrell and Nathan. Nathan turns her way and waves. Lexie turns to her and motions toward the office. Woo Woo looks at Lexie. Looks at Nathan. Dear God, how could she have been so blind.

Jaxx hears the participants leaving the yoga studio. He stiffens. Reminds himself he can wrap Kristi around his little finger. Always could. This time it might take a little longer, but it's foolproof. A smile here, a casual hand on her back, a downward glance to show humility. Jaxx has always had this power, over men and women, but mostly women. It will not fail him now.

In anticipation of Kristi's arrival Jaxx looks out the office door. He wants to be ready. What he does not want is to see Detective Numb Nuts in the gym talking to one of his personal trainers. Jaxx starts to rise. He'll put an end to this. Before he can push the chair away from himself, he sits back down. Now is not the time to worry about the cop or his idle threats. At least Jaxx hopes they're idle. That's an issue for another time. Now he must focus on Kristi and getting back in her good graces.

That is not going to happen. Jaxx knows that when Charlene walks into the office with Kristi. He tries to tell himself he still has this. The situation is under control. The pit of his stomach says differently.

Kristi wastes no time. She has rehearsed this. She has gone through numerous scenarios in her mind. She has explored potential outcomes. Kristi is done. She wants this shit over with, come what may.

"Jaxx, we need to terminate our business relationship. I've drawn up a contract." Charlene steps forward and hands Jaxx a document. He looks down at the papers and up at Kristi. Charlene swears he twinkled like the star on a Christmas tree. Good God, is he flirting?

"I'll give you ten minutes to read the contract. Then I'll answer any questions. Then you'll sign. Then this will be done." Kristi sweeps her hands across the office and points to the gym. Then she sits down. Charlene joins her.

The women wait. Jaxx is looking at the document but he's not reading it. He's trying to determine what his next move should be. Charm didn't work. He can do as he was asked but he doesn't like where that might lead. He can refuse to take part in this charade and storm out. Jaxx really does storm out of a room well. I mean what could Kristi do?

For the second time in the last few minutes Jaxx starts to rise out of his chair. At that moment, like the gods have aligned, Terrell sticks his head in the door. "Sorry to interrupt. Just wanted to let Charlene and Kristi know we'll be in the café." Terrell nods at Jaxx. Charlene swears the detective twinkled.

Jaxx starts reading. There's little doubt he's screwed. If he signs the termination contract, he's out of the business, out on his ass, and out of any money he hoped would be coming his way. If he doesn't sign the contract, he could end up in jail. At the very least, he'll end up in a long and protracted legal action, which will hurt his reputation and his wallet. It would also hurt Kristi's reputation and her wallet. Jaxx considers this second option carefully.

"You have one minute," Kristi says. Charlene checks her watch. Jaxx flips them both the bird.

"Time's up," Kristi says. "Do you have any questions?"

"Yeah, when did you become such a bitch?"

Charlene rises. "I'll get Detective Terrell."

Kristi motions Charlene back down. "This is bravado. It's what Jaxx does when he doesn't have another move." Kristi remains perfectly still. She breathes in and out. She pictures herself moving through a vinyasa flow from forward fold to halfway lift to plank to downward dog. She breathes in. There is nothing in the pit of her stomach.

Kristi has taken her eyes off the outside world and moved inward. She is too slow to react when Jaxx suddenly stands up something in his hand. Charlene has not gone inward. She has her eyes glued to Jaxx. When he throws the contract – the signed contract – at Kristi's face she jumps forward and grabs it.

Jaxx is already out the door. "Bitch," he yells over his shoulder. And storms out.

Kristi watches Jaxx exit. She has been doing yoga and meditation for as long as she can remember. It is part of the fabric of her life, and she sees its benefits run deeply through her core. She knows joy, she knows gratitude, she knows forgiveness. She thinks of all of this now in the split seconds that Jaxx walks over the threshold and out of her life. She does what her heart tells her is right.

"Bite me!" Kristi yells at the ass end of the man who was once her business partner.

Charlene is regaling the café crowd with what happened in the office – with Kristi's aplomb, her fortitude, her resolve. Everyone is beaming. When Charlene gets to the part where Kristi yells, "Bite me," everyone applauds.

A voice behind them says, "Well, if I knew I was going to get that reaction, I'd come more often." Everyone looks up to see Jennifer Boone. Charlene wonders if this is going to become a regular thing. Lexie wonders if she's gay. Terrell wonders what the hell is wrong.

Woo Woo moves over on the sofa and indicates a spot for Boone. Charlene, at everyone's request, retells the story of Jaxx's exit from Vitality+. Boone applauds. Woo Woo beams. So does Kristi. She's trying to remind herself about gratitude and forgiveness, and humility. But she quite likes bite-me Kristi. So do her friends.

The group moves on to other topics – vaccination shots, Ryan Reynolds, the benefits of amethyst – until it's time to move up and out. Kristi heads back to her office, her company. Lexie is about to record a podcast, and Charlene is scurrying to walk Madoff. He will be irritated. Terrell and Boone remain in their seats.

"What's up?" Terrell asks.

"We had our monthly statistics meeting."

"Oof. Bet that made an enema look pleasurable."

Boone laughs. "The numbers are never good enough for the posse. I told them we are about to close a number of cases, including the missing Nautilus. Hope I wasn't lying."

Terrell shrugs. Boone shifts in her seat and hands over her phone. "Did you see this? Thought you'd find it interesting."

"It" turned out to be an item in CityNews. The results of the Bluenose

Marathon Two. Terrell looks at his boss and raises his eyebrows. "Check out twelfth place."

In twelfth place is Abby Downton. Terrell lets out a little hoot. "Who knew. Last time I saw her she was drinking a mojito and reading something called *The Thong Principle*."

"It appears she also runs marathons. Successfully."

"She's faster than me," Terrell agrees, looking at Downton's time. Three hours and twenty-six minutes.

"You think Newhouse has seen this?"

"Who knows? Maybe. If he has, one thing's for sure. He'll be annoyed." Boone shoots him a questioning look. "Newhouse doesn't like to be outdone. Even if he didn't run the race."

"And yet he picks her to have an affair with. He has a type." Boone looks at Terrell and grins. "Most men do. Except you, apparently."

The joke is lost on Terrell. He's running Boone's previous comment through his mind and wondering why it took him so long to see what was right in front of his face. Like a domino run the pieces are falling into place. Boone takes one look at Terrell and knows what's going on. She has worked with the detective for more than 20 years. She's seen this look before. She knows better than to interrupt. Boone reaches for her phone and checks her email. After about five minutes, Terrell gets aimlessly up from his chair and makes his way to the counter. He comes back with two herbal teas. Boone's tastes like a flower and smells like raspberry. Her friend has got it bad, she thinks.

Terrell takes a sip of his tea – some pale green thing that smells like lavender – and shakes his head. He looks at his cup like he's never seen it before.

"You know who stole Newhouse's watch don't you?"

"I do," says Terrell, "what I don't know is how to prove it."

"All circumstantial?"

"Yep. It all adds up; all the pieces fit. Except there is no evidence."

"Do you think you could scare it out of them? Bring them into interrogation?"

"Newhouse has a type, remember. Abby Downton wouldn't break if we waterboarded her. No, we're going to have to be clever. We going to have to get them off kilter."

"Oh well, if it's clever you want," says Boone, "ask your newfound friends."

Terrell has one question he can ask. One question that will further cement his theory, what his gut knows to be true. He heads over to the gym. Nathan is standing behind the front desk. Just the man Terrell wants. He makes chitchat for a few seconds, but Nathan isn't falling for this again. "What do you want?"

"Quick question. Who takes towels into the changerooms?"

Nathan is confused. He's already answered this question. "We all do. Whoever has a free minute restocks the shelves and takes out the dirty laundry."

"Let me be more specific. Do you ever take towels into the women's changeroom?"

Nathan is pretty sure the detective is losing it. He nods yes and takes a step back. "Let me be more specific," says Terrell, "do women ever change the towels in the men's changeroom?"

Terrell thinks he may have to resuscitate Nathan. Clearly brains and brawn. Since he's on a roll Terrell decides to throw out one more question. "What's up with you and Lexie?"

Nathan speaks so softly Terrell has to lean in. Even then he's not sure he's heard correctly. He looks directly at Nathan, who nods. "Jesus."

* * *

The smell of sausage and cheese and oregano fills the kitchen and wends its way to the dining room. Madoff takes a deep breath. He likes it when company comes to dinner. There are often leftovers and sometimes, when Mama C. isn't looking, he gets treats right from the table. It's not begging, he tells himself. It's being in the right place at the right time. Today was an especially good day. Not only is company coming, but he got to go in the car – all the way to Dartmouth. On the way home, as usual, when they turn onto Nelson's Landing Road, Mama C rolls down the window and Madoff gets to stick his head outside. They drive very slowly so Madoff can look around the neighborhood. He's the prettiest dog on the block.

While Madoff salivates, Charlene sets the table and gets out the wine glasses. She pours a glass for herself, a dusky pinot blanc with hints of elderberry, or so she read on Vivino. She really doesn't know what it means. She doesn't even know what an elderberry is. Nor does she care. Tonight is too important to fuss with the nuances of wine, and she can safely say Lexie and Woo Woo don't care. Although Woo Woo may own a winery in France. Who knows.

What Charlene does know is that her proposal must be persuasive. Charlene believes she is most persuasive when she has a PowerPoint presentation. And she does. Something tells Charlene though that this is not the right group or the right proposition for PPTX. Without her slide deck though, Charlene feels a little adrift. Like an accountant without a calculator.

The women come together. They have to spend some time cooing over Madoff, rubbing his belly and getting licked, then they head right for the kitchen. "Something smells delicious," Lexie says breathing in deeply. Madoff loves Aunt Lexie.

Lexie and Woo Woo know that Charlene wants to talk to them about something. Lexie's tendency is to dive right in and ask what tonight is all about. Woo Woo knows Lexie is blunt. She also knows this isn't about being dismissive or rude. It's about being Lexie. On the drive over, she suggested they wait for Charlene to bring up whatever it is she wants to talk to them about. Lexie shot Woo Woo a knowing look. "Got it. Keep my mouth shut."

The cannelloni is superb, moist and rich without being heavy. There is a green salad with an assortment of fixings – grated cheeses, Craisins, shaved almonds, croutons – and garlic bread. Everyone dives in. To Madoff's amazement, Woo Woo puts a small plate of cannelloni at the end of the table for him, and Mama C. doesn't say a word. Madoff loves Aunt Woo Woo.

The three women are having a great time. Lexie realizes it's been a while since she has relaxed with friends. Since dining out has been about being together and not about work or ratings or subscribers. Woo Woo is having such a pleasant evening she indulges in another glass of wine. She looks at her friends. She can feel the tears in her eyes. She picks up Madoff and gives him a cuddle. Madoff swears Aunt Woo Woo just wiped her eyes on his back. He forgives her. The empty cannelloni plate is still on the floor. Charlene knows everyone is enjoying themselves. She hopes the festive atmosphere continues and wonders once again if she should use her PPTX slides.

Dessert is gelato. There are three kinds: lemon, pistachio, and fior di latte. Everyone scoops up the flavors they want into their angoily ice cream bowls. (Charlene can't wait to tell everyone she bought them at the Dollarama.) To Madoff's amazement, a small scoop of fior di latte, or milk flower, is placed on the floor. He turns to give Aunt Woo Woo a lick and realizes it's not Woo Woo who put the bowl on the floor. It's Mama C. Madoff thinks this may be the best day of his life.

There's decaf coffee and herbal tea. And there's no more stalling. Charlene thinks perhaps she should get the PPTX. Before she can move, she feels a hand on hers. It's Woo Woo. "We're all ears."

Here goes, thinks Charlene to herself. Nothing ventured, nothing gained. Charlene, with Kristi's permission, shares what she knows about Vitality+ as a business. It's more than viable. Membership is growing in double digits year over year and the gym's retention rate is twenty-eight percent higher than the national average. (Charlene has done her homework.) That's the plus side. On the downside is Jaxx. They may never know how long Jaxx has been bilking the business, or for how much, but the company is now in the red. It will take a few years before black ink emerges;

however, the potential for growth and profit is significant.

"That sounds good for Kristi," says Lexie. "She'll be able to keep the business."

"Yes and no," says Charlene. "Kristi needs cash flow now. She could get a loan if she had collateral. She doesn't."

"That leaves investors," says Woo Woo. "That's why we're here."

"It is," Charlene acknowledges.

"The auditor and the heiress will have to explain to me what's going on. I have no idea," says Lexie.

Charlene spells it out for her – the idea that has kept her from going to bed at Madoff's appointed hour, the idea that excites her and terrifies her. It comes down to this: let's invest in Vitality+. Let's become the co-owners of a gym that also has a yoga studio.

There are dozens of questions from Lexie and Woo Woo. Most Charlene can answer – how much would each of them have to contribute; when would they take over; what would their role, or roles, be exactly; would they have to work at the gym – although most of the answers are not specific.

"Everything is up for discussion," says Charlene, 'but we don't have to commit to anything until we are one hundred percent comfortable with the terms."

What Charlene is not hearing and what had worried her most are these four words: I can't afford it. She is hearing interest on two levels: investing in a business because of the potential return on investment and investing as a way of helping Kristi.

"That is a bit of a wrinkle," says Charlene. She feels three sets of eyes on her. (Madoff senses something is up.) "I haven't mentioned this to Kristi."

"No need to get her hopes up or insult her if we aren't all in," says Woo Woo. She looks at Lexie and Charlene, even Madoff. This is friendship. Money is not an issue for her, and she has no doubt this proposal is not an attempt to get money out of her. That realization is foreign to Woo Woo. She is used to being cautious with whom she lets inside her world. There are lots of colleagues, clients, acquaintances. Woo Woo isn't sure she has many true friends, if any. She does now.

"I'm in," says Woo Woo.

Now the eyes are on Lexie. "We could make the gym LGBTQ friendly. I could start a new podcast or have a monthly recording from the gym. I could have an office in the gym, which could be a tax deduction and a way to increase revenue for the gym."

"We could have a bring-your-dog-to-the gym day," says Charlene. Then she breaks into tears. Woo Woo pats her hand. Woo Woo's phone rings. She has no intention of answering it until she sees the caller's name displayed. Michael Terrell.

Lexie and Charlene are just as curious. Woo Woo answers.

"Are you on speaker phone?" Terrell asks.

"I am now," says Woo Woo. "Is everything alright?"

Terrell doesn't answer that question. He asks another. "Are Lexie and Charlene with you?"

"Yes," says Woo Woo. The other women say hello.

"Can I come over?" Terrell asks.

Madoff is confused. Suddenly the women are pushing back their chairs and clearing the table. There is a flurry of activity. Madoff was enjoying an after-gelato nap. He follows everyone into the kitchen. Perhaps the guests are leaving. Perhaps he will get to bed on time tonight.

Nope. The kettle is back on, the plate of pastries refreshed, and another plate and cup taken out of the cupboard. In the melee to clear the clutter, Lexie scrapes some leftovers onto a plate. Absently, she puts the plate on the floor. Madoff nonchalantly walks toward the plate. Best day ever.

It takes Terrell about fifteen minutes to get to Charlene's house. He stopped on the way to buy a bottle of wine as a thank you. He arrives, wine and apology in hand. It's almost nine o'clock. The first words out of Woo Woo's mouth. "Are you okay?" The first words out of Charlene's mouth. "Have you eaten?" The first words out of Lexie's mouth. "Is that wine for us?"

The three women are sitting around the dining room table drinking wine and smiling, just a hint of concern at the corners of their mouths. Terrell is digging into some delicious cannelloni. Madoff at his heels. "Tell me about your evening first."

The three women look at each other. They nod. "We're going to offer to become investors in Vitality+."

"Wow," says Terrell. "Great idea. You could have a day or time for police officers to come and work out. They'd like that."

Charlene makes a note. (She's started a notebook called Marketing.) Woo Woo refills the wine glasses. Lexie leans across the table. "You're stalling."

That's exactly what Terrell is doing. This seemed like such a great idea when his boss suggested it. It seemed like a solid idea when he called. It even seemed like a good idea when he stopped at the NSLC for wine. Now that his belly is full, the women are staring at him, and the dog is in his lap, he's not so sure.

"It's okay. Safe space," says Woo Woo.

Terrell knows what she means although he doesn't know why he should. This is a new world to him. He's just trying to keep up. He's also aware he has never done anything like this in his thirty-odd years with the police department. This is either brilliant or debauched. It's either going to lead to a criminal behind bars or egg on his face. "I'm here to ask a favor."

"Really?" says Lexie. "You've asked favors of us before and you haven't gotten your knickers in a twist."

"This favor requires me to do something I'm not comfortable with, something my superiors – those way up the food chain – may not be comfortable with."

"You know who stole the watch," says Charlene. Everyone looks at her in surprise, more because the words came out of Charlene's mouth and not Woo Woo's.

"I know who the thief is," Terrell admits, "and I don't know how to ask this favor without telling you who it is."

"Try," says Woo Woo. She knows what it's like to walk an ethical line and fall off the edge. "If you can't ask us without naming the thief, then we'll deal with that when it comes up."

Terrell is impressed. Just might work. "Okay, we have a thief. We have motive and opportunity. We have means. What we don't have is evidence. Or rather, we have circumstantial evidence."

"And you can't break this person." Charlene knows she has been watching too many cop shows, but Madoff enjoys them.

"No," Terrell agrees with a grin, "I don't think this person can be bullied or cajoled into confessing their crime." He turns to Lexie. "Nathan would break in under five minutes." Lexie feels a tear running down her cheek. She leans forward and Madoff licks it off for her.

"How can we help?" Charlene asks.

"I need to disorient this person. I need to throw them off their game. Then I need to interrogate them."

So, it's a woman, Charlene thinks. "So, it's a woman," Lexie says out loud. Charlene and Woo Woo shoot her a look.

"There's a fifty-fifty chance you're right," says Terrell. He finds he is enjoying himself. This really might work.

"And you'd like us to do what exactly?" says Charlene. "Disorient this person."

"Yes, please," says Terrell.

"That will require more wine," says Lexie. She stands up.

"White is in the fridge, red in the wine rack in the pantry," Charlene calls after her.

They are now two bottles in. Charlene has brought out a flipchart from her office. She has colored markers. Among the suggestions for how she and her friends could help disorient the thief:

> Accuse the person outright. Imply they aren't the only ones that know this person is guilty.
> Break into the person's house and search for the watch. (Not all ideas are legal. Hence the colored markers.)
> Tell the person you would be willing to buy some jewelry from them. Nudge, nudge. Wink, wink.

Follow this person to see where they might have hidden the watch.

Tell Newhouse you know who the thief is and have him throw a hissy fit at the gym. (Not all ideas are good for business. Hence the colored markers.)

Start working out at the gym to eavesdrop and learn more. (Not all ideas are good for the spirit. Hence ....)

Plant the second watch on the thief.

Invite the thief out for drinks and get them drunk.

Perhaps refreshments will help. Woo Woo gets up to put a pot of decaf coffee on. Charlene prepares a plate of cheese and crackers. Terrell is taking Madoff for his nightly constitutional. Lexie hands him the leash.

Terrell looks at her. Maybe it's the wine. "You need to talk to Nathan."

The coffee, food, and fresh air does everyone a world of good. They are unanimous. Their ideas for disruption suck. Most are not practical, some are not legal, none are good. None are going to get them the results Terrell needs.

"Well, we tried," says Terrell. "I appreciate your help and giving up most of your evening for this." It's nearly midnight. Madoff has given up on ever getting to bed on time.

Everyone sighs. No one likes defeat. Woo Woo hesitates for just a second. "It would drive Ariel nuts if she had to spend time with Newhouse's ex. We could have his former lover set up an appointment with Ariel for personal training."

Terrell stops mid-double take. Of course, Woo Woo knows who the thief is, Terrell thinks. And now she is not alone. Once Woo Woo puts the name out there, Lexie and Charlene see the pieces for themselves. No one asks Woo Woo how she knew. Could be logic. Could be something else. No one wants to know. No one needs to know. That's what friends are for.

Woo Woo's idea has merit. Abby would undoubtedly flaunt her relationship with Newhouse. She might even flaunt how profitable that relationship was for her. It would get under Ariel's skin. Indeed, it would get under anyone's skin. Two potential problems. One, will Abby do it? Two, will she need to know Ariel stole the watch? Terrell is hoping it's yes to the former and no to the latter.

It's too late to call Abby now. In fact, as Terrell checks his watch, he realizes it's past midnight. He'll hit the hay and call Abby first thing in the morning. The women agree to stay away from Ariel and not leak anything to Kristi if Terrell keeps them in the loop. They gather up the remaining dishes on the dining room table and take them to the kitchen. Lexie scoops up Madoff and puts him, gently, in his doggy bed.

The women decide tomorrow it will be yoga as usual. They'll need to reach out to Kristi, but first they need to decide exactly what it is they're going to offer. What is it they want and what is fair to everyone involved. The reality is that for each of them the motivation to buy into Vitality+ is unique. Lexie is looking for profile and roots. Charlene wants purpose and a challenge. Woo Woo wants to support her friends. She might also want to teach a meditation class in her own yoga studio, or perhaps reflexology. They agree to meet at Lexie's for brunch on Sunday.

There are yawns and hugs at the door. Terrell thanks the women for their help and their discretion. A sharp sound in the background prompts them to exit quietly and quickly. Madoff is ready for the big bed.

Madoff is about to be disappointed. Mama C. has picked him up and slathered him with kisses, as it should be. Her pajamas are on, and Madoff is nestled on his side of the bed. Now Mama C. should reach for the light. To turn it off. Instead, she reaches for her notebook. First, she turns to look at the little light of her life. This is not Madoff's routine and Madoff loves his routine. Charlene has come prepared. She reaches into the pocket of her pajama bottoms, sprinkled with images of Westies, and brings out a chew stick. Madoff can't believe it. Food on the bed! A chewstick before sleep!

Best day ever.

It's past midnight and I'm still awake. I can't believe it. Madoff can't believe it. But he can be bought off with a chewstick. I'm not sure the vet would approve, but Madoff and I agree this is the best option for ending a long day that is not yet over.

I'm amazed. The girls embraced the idea of buying into Vitality+. I thought I might be able to persuade them. They didn't even need to be convinced. I think not using the PPTX was a good idea.

We are all on the same page. Each of us might have different reasons for saying yes, but we're in this together. There is a real sense of wanting to do this. Together. That's the truth. I'm not interested in being co-owner of a gym if I can't own it with Lexie and Woo Woo. (And Kristi.)

Truth be told, I'm more than amazed at how well tonight went. I'm excited. That's why I'm lying here wide-eyed. A new business. A new business in a sector I've never worked in before. I'm not going into this ill-informed or inexperienced though. I know business. I know what is required for success. I see that in Vitality+. And if it doesn't work out, so be it. I still have investments, and I'm still doing some consulting. I will not suffer financially. Neither will Woo Woo or Lexie. It's a win-win as tax accountants like to say. Like anyone but the government ever wins when it comes to taxes.

I'm more than excited though. I'm looking forward to what comes next. It's been a long time since I've felt this way. Since tomorrow held more promise than predictability. Since there was a reason to get up that wasn't sadly familiar and reflective of the day before and the day before. Not that I'm feeling sorry for myself. My life is good. I have my children, my profession. I have Madoff. Now I have a gym.

Well, I hope I have a gym. Kristi might say no. I don't think she will. We can make the terms appealing to her and favorable to everyone. This isn't about taking advantage of a business opportunity and it isn't about helping a friend. It's both, and it's more.

If I'm being honest, friendship might be the best thing about owning Vitality+. I have friends, of course, but I have discovered they are invariably work friends. Now that I'm not working full time, running an auditing department, attending events, going to meetings, and being seen, I'm not often connecting with my professional friends. I like them, sure, and I'm certain they like me, but our worlds overlap less and less. Lexie and Woo Woo are different. I doubt they can read a spreadsheet.

I think we will continue to be friends even if we don't buy the gym, but this venture unites us in a way brunch at the Almonak never could. (Perhaps monthly brunch meetings could be our thing.) We're also connected to the gym because we're connected to Kristi, we helped purloin (look it up) data from Jaxx's computer, we helped draw information out of the police on a podcast, we helped devise a plot to trap a thief. We have been busy. And we didn't break a sweat.

If I'm still being honest, I need to figure out how deep this new friendship will go. How deep a vein I'm willing to open. It is not my nature to invite people into the shadows of my world. You'd think Dora would know that. She called yesterday. On and on again about connecting with my past, with those who have gone before me. I truly don't give a hoot. Maybe I should. I don't. I don't know why Dora is pushing this. Is she looking for me to tell her, again, what a great gift she gave me? Does she want me to marry my first cousin? Why can't she leave me alone.

Now I'm in a bind. Tell Dora about him and listen to her go on endlessly about how I must call him. Must connect. Must embrace him and my new reality. Good God. I'm weary just thinking about it.

Don't tell Dora and I get to feel guilty. Guilty I didn't tell Dora and guilty I didn't call him. 'Cause let's face it, the only reason I wouldn't tell Dora is because I didn't call him. I also won't tell Dora I don't like her gift.

Maybe I will at some point. That point will only happen if I call him. I don't want to call him. I don't want to know he even exists.
Sincerely,
Charlene Kurtz
PS I'm still excited.
PSS I think Madoff just farted.

Chapter 22.

There are times the element of surprise works in one's favor. Terrell is hoping this is one of those times. Abby Downton answers the door on the second ring.

"Assuming this is not a social call." She walks ahead. Terrell follows. "Might as well join me for coffee." Terrell accepts the cup and takes a sip. It's delicious. Hot, fresh, dark.

"First one today?" Abby asks. Terrell nods. He looks around the condo. Neat. Everything in its place. *The Thong Principle* is still on the coffee table in the living room, although the bookmark has moved deeper into the pages. There is no mojito in sight.

"So, you need a favor." Abby is scanning his face. Terrell did not realize he was that easy to read. "You have everything you need to know that I didn't steal the watch, and yet here you are. This should be interesting."

Terrell tries to make it sound more routine than interesting. He explains they'd like to observe reactions in the gym, and no one can get quite the reactions Ms. Downton can. Abby laughs. It's one of those deep, genuine laughs that resonates throughout a room and through a body.

"You want me to catch a thief."

"No." Terrell is clear on this. "I do not want you to catch a thief. I do not want you to mention the watch. I do not want you in any way to look for clues or play detective. I will do that."

"You just want me to stand there and look good. I can do that."

"I was hoping you'd spend a bit of time with a personal trainer."

"Your choice of trainer or mine?"

"Mine."

"Will Dick Wadd be there?"

"I don't know. He might be."

"Got it. You don't think he stole his own watch."

"I think your presence at the gym will have the effect we desire. Just be yourself."

The laugh is back. This time Terrell joins in.

The group has nominated Charlene to invite Kristi for tea and treats on Saturday. There will be no "We'd like to talk with you about something," or "We have an idea we'd like to run by you." Simply, come to tea. It's an Atlantic Canadian thing. Kristi won't think it too out of the ordinary, and she just might be glad to have the company.

The wording of this invitation required a lot of discussion. Say, "We have an idea, come to tea," and Kristi thinks the only reason she is being invited is because they want something, which is true. And not true. However, if they only say, "Come to tea," Kristi might feel ambushed when they unveil their idea.

Over tea, coffee, and something with whipped cream that Lexie slurped back at the café, the women decided the best course of action is to read the room when they are all in the room. If they get the sense Kristi needs companionship, they'll broach the idea at another time. If they get the sense Kristi is worried about money, they'll put their idea forward as a possible solution.

Until Kristi says yes, the group is in a holding pattern. They decide moving forward – speaking with a lawyer, drafting an agreement among the three of them, talking with their respective bankers – would be both preemptive and disrespectful to Kristi. Woo Woo says it would also be a jinx.

No one wants that.

Lexie has very little to do to prepare for Saturday. She has stocked up on tea, some organic stuff Woo Woo recommended. Madoff is also coming, so Lexie has dog treats and ice cream. She'll go the European bakery in the morning and pick up something delicious and non-organic. She wonders if she should invite her friends to stay for a light supper after Kristi leaves. There is something she wants to talk to them about.

There is something she is afraid to talk to them about.

* * *

No one slept soundly Friday night. Well, Madoff did, but everyone else lay awake thinking about how events could possibly go wrong tomorrow, or tossing and turning thinking about how events could possibly go very wrong tomorrow.

Terrell is taking a risk. He knows that. But rock, hard place. He needs to nudge Ariel so she'll slip up. She's not a master criminal. She got lucky. She took a watch when no one was looking, and no one thought twice about a trainer taking fresh towels into a changeroom and dirty laundry out. He's not sure if she wants to get the money for the watch – feels entitled to it as another of Byron Newhouse's toss-away women – or if this is just revenge for promises unfulfilled and lies smoothly spoken.

It doesn't matter her motivation, or her intent. Everything points to Ariel except concrete evidence. There are no fingerprints on the locker or the lock, except for Newhouse's. Terrell wouldn't expect any. Ariel likely wore gloves, not unusual if you're doing a quick clean of a changeroom. The key was never found, probably tossed or flushed. Ariel would know where to look for the key, maybe even had a copy made during

245

one of the times Newhouse couldn't "find" his. If that's the case, Ariel has been planning this for some time.

That's not likely, Terrell thinks. The downward spiral started when Abby showed up and revealed Newhouse for the letch he is. Doesn't leave a lot of time to hatch a plan and copy a key. And if she copied the key, where did Newhouse's second key go? No, Ariel took it, and she took it to get inside Newhouse's locker. Terrell isn't quite sure how she got her hands on the key, but it's widely acknowledged Newhouse left it lying around everywhere or falling out of his Gymshark shorts.

The detective is also certain Newhouse has no idea Ariel stole his watch. He thinks it's Christian, doesn't think his fling has the temerity or the wherewithal to defy him. Terrell is less certain what Newhouse would do, scratch that, will do when he finds out. It may be worth $60,000 to him to keep this from his wife and kid.

There's no doubt though that Ariel is the thief. Terrell is so sure of this he's told Boone. She thinks his plan is risky, but there are no other options.

There is also no chance of any sleep. Terrell gets up and showers. He needs to be at the gym when Abby is finished with Ariel, but he can't be seen hanging around. That would get Ariel's guard up. So, Terrell is taking a yoga class. He thinks he took one or two in university, maybe as a recruit. He's not quite sure what to wear and opts for sweats and a t-shirt. You can never go wrong with sweats.

Terrell arrives fifteen minutes early. Abby won't arrive for another 30 minutes, and her training session will end at roughly the same time as the yoga class. Woo Woo gives him the all-clear signal when Ariel steps into the lunchroom, and he makes his way quickly to the studio. Woo Woo, Lexie, and Charlene do not usually take weekend classes, but they aren't missing this for anything.

Kristi has set up a practice area for Terrell: mat, strap, bolster, and blocks. He's between two people he's never met before and staring across the studio at the triumvirate. Most people are stretching or deep breathing, perhaps meditating. Terrell is familiar with warming-up. Cops are expected to pass annual physicals. Terrell aces his. He is being careful not to show up the people in the room. He is considerate like that.

Kristi plays a single chord on her iPhone and everyone comes to a seat on the mat. She introduces two newcomers to the group, including Terrell. Some people wave, some nod, a few say welcome. Terrell is really glad he didn't go all out with his warm-up.

They begin on their backs with some breathwork and a short visualization. There is also a mantra. Terrell thought he would be restless, even dismissive, but he feels his body starting to relax. When Kristi tells everyone to release their jaw, Terrell realizes his is clenched.

From the opening breathwork and centering, Kristi takes them through some twists and balances in table. There is something called cat/cow. Terrell enjoys this. He sees why people like yoga. Everyone is now standing tall, positioning their right foot at an angle behind them and moving into warrior one and two. Terrell has seen these in movies.

Then it's downward dog. Terrell is trying not to stand out with his prowess. Kristi suggests everyone bend their knees, then straighten them. Terrell's downward dog stretches higher. His back is straighter, his head better positioned between his arms. Who knew.

Next, it's plank and what Kristi calls chaturanga. Terrell calls this a push-up. He sees several people struggle. He remains modest. He should know better. From plank it's back to downward dog. Kristi tells everyone to stand on their tippy toes, bend and jump to the top of the mat. Several people do this. A few attempt it. Some just walk to the top of the mat. Terrell falls on his ass.

It's all downhill from here. Terrell can't move his foot to his groin for tree pose and can't keep it on his calf and remain still. He ends up placing his foot on the floor and leaning it against his ankle. He looks at Woo

Woo, right leg strong and straight, left leg at a forty-five-degree angle to her groin. Her eyes riveted at some spot on the floor. He wonders if it might be a bug.

From tree pose they move to warrior three. Terrell prefers its predecessors. He stumbles. Then it's upright once more and to the pose of the week: bird of paradise. Terrell is a strong man, he's physically fit, and he's agile. More than once he's had to dive for cover, usually from an angry family member. This bird eludes him. One leg is supposed to lift, one arm is supposed to go under the uplifted leg. And you're supposed to smile. Almost everyone is struggling, but everyone is also trying. So does Terrell. He's beginning to like yoga.

Now for a resting pose: child's pose. He smiles at Woo Woo as she folds herself into a ball, one with the floor and her breath. He joins her. He folds. There is no ball. He folds once more. His ass tells him to never do that again.

At last, savasana. Terrell collapses. He closes his eyes, gratefully. He can hear Kristi moving quietly about the room. He feels her above him. She bends down and places two cotton rounds on his eyes. They smell like heaven. Kristi tells everyone the oils are lavender and cedarwood. Then she has them relax different parts of the body one at a time. Terrell feels the difference before and after. He breathes in heaven. A bell rings and

Kristi brings them back to this space and the present.

Terrell is limp.

* * *

It's a glorious fall day. The sun is bright, the air is warm, and the leaves are hanging on for one last splurge of color. Ariel feels, for the first time in many weeks, a skip in her step. The corners of her mouth turn up. She walks through the doors of Vitality+ looking forward to the day ahead.

Ariel grabs a coffee in the lunchroom. Some fair trade, organic, monkey-adjacent blend that checks all the right boxes. Kristi must have bought it. Of course, Kristi is buying everything now. She spent some time talking with the staff about Jaxx leaving and reassuring them everything would be fine. Business as usual.

No one really knows why Jaxx left. There are a number of theories: lover's spat, ill health, rehab. Personally, Ariel thinks it's because Jaxx got tapped to step up and pull his weight around the gym. No pun intended. Jaxx was good with clients, and easy to look at, but lazy as sin. While everyone else saw to the running of the business, Jaxx would spend hours in his office on the computer. Maybe he has a porn addiction.

Coffee in hand, and the corners of her mouth still upturned, Ariel makes her way to the front desk. She waves at a few clients coming in the door. Saturdays can be busy. Ariel checks her schedule. Four sessions today. That's a good day. The first session is with a new client. Those are either very enjoyable or very difficult. Ariel checks the name: Abigail. No last name. Not that Ariel needs one. She'll get that on intake.

There is a sound. Ariel can't quite place it. It may be coming from behind her or to her left. It's coming from her. Ariel realizes she is humming and chuckles. Things are looking up. This is going to be a good day.

Exercise bands. Wrist weights. Foam mat. Ariel decides she'll concentrate the first training session on the floor. Avoid the equipment. Floor exercises will help her to get to know the client and start building a relationship. That's the key to repeat business.

The whoosh of the front door alerts Ariel. Likely her client. She turns, the corners of her mouth upward, her eyes bright. A tall slim blonde walks in. She has a big smile on her face and a confident stride. She sees Ariel across the room and waves. Ariel swears the smile gets bigger. Ariel waves back, not as enthusiastically as her client. There is something about this woman ...

Jesus H.

Ariel reminds herself she is a professional. This is what she does for a living. She doesn't have to like her clients; she doesn't need to be besties with them. She needs to help them attain their fitness goals. Abby Downton's goals are quite simple: to stay in shape and stay healthy. That must have taken a lot of thought.

No, Ariel tells herself. Don't go there. Don't delve into snark. Byron can sleep with whomever he wants. No business of hers. She's done with the loser. Can't even hold on to his own watch. The corners of Ariel's mouth lift once more.

Clients fall into one of three groups: fanatics, friends, fools. The former have a singular focus on their exercise regimen. They're usually men, and they're usually very competitive. This would be Newhouse and his ilk. The second category is usually women, and they want to stay in shape, to get fitter, faster, stronger. They also feel this overwhelming need to be polite, to make conversation, to talk about their life. Ariel prefers group one. Trainers don't generally like group three. These are the people, men, women, and everyone else on the human spectrum, that have convinced themselves they want to be physically fit. They likely convince themselves of this once a decade and they join a gym. It is a waste of money. These people want to be in shape; they don't want to get in shape. That requires work and commitment. Not a discussion of what you did at the gym today over soy lattes.

Group one. That's where Ariel would place Abby, as she has been told with a hint of glee to call her client. Her muscles are well defined; she can do thirty squats and not be out of breath. Those are signs of someone who is serious about fitness. Yet Abby wants to chat. She wants to know all about the gym and all about Ariel. She also wants to apologize.

"I'm so sorry for my appearance a few weeks ago. It was embarrassing, but I was so upset."

Ariel feigns ignorance.

Abby pivots. "Do you know Byron?"

Ariel nods.

"Then you know he can be an ass."

Ariel tries not to smile. She fails. Abby catches the grin, and they are fast friends.

"I shouldn't tell you this, but why not. That man slept in my bed for three years. Well, he didn't do much sleeping." Abby preens.

Ariel feels something in her stomach. It may be nausea.

"The whole time we were together he told me he was going to leave his wife. Told me he loved me. Told me I was his love bug. Can you believe that? The words 'love bug' coming out of Byron Newhouse's mouth?"

Ariel can, actually. She races for the washroom. Abby continues to lunge.

Ariel wipes vomit off her mouth. She rinses her mouth with mouthwash. She splashes some water on her face. She's thinking how she will explain this to Abby. Sudden flu perhaps. Migraine. Ariel has heard migraines cause queasiness. Food poisoning. She decides to wing it.

The staff washroom door closes behind Ariel. She starts walking toward Abby. She thinks it would be good to give her a thumbs up. But Abby is not looking at her. She's looking across the room. The yoga group is starting to exit. Ariel recognizes Lexie, and Charlene, and Woo Woo. And …

Jesus H.

Terrell rolls to the right and breathes in for a count of three. Then he makes his way to a seated position, eyes still closed. Kristi ends the class with the mantra. *I find happiness from within. I share my happiness with others.* Before Terrell can open his eyes and rise, gingerly, a water bottle is in his hands.

"How are you feeling?" Woo Woo asks.

"Like I've just gone twelve rounds with Muhammad Ali."

"Ahh, that would be the binds. It will get easier."

"Something to look forward to," says Terrell. A small part of him means it. Before the detective exits the studio, he takes his shield and clasps it to the waistband of his sweats where it can't be missed. Everyone in the class certainly sees it.

As Terrell leaves the studio behind and enters the gym, he looks up to see Ariel. She is not looking at him. She's looking at Abby, and Abby is looking at him. He's not sure what is going on. Ariel looks terrified. Abby looks deep in thought.

It doesn't matter how anyone looks or what those looks might mean. Terrell heads directly for Ariel. She is like a deer caught in headlights: immobile. The detective can sense her desire to run, but she remains rooted. Abby, however, is on the move. She grabs her gear and rushes out of the gym.

Ariel watches Terrell coming closer, and closer. He's in front of her. She says the only thing and the first thing that comes to her mind.

"Prick."

Terrell has been called worse, much worse, and many of those names came from people supposed to be on his side. He treats the profanity with the attention it deserves, absolutely none.

"I'd like to talk with you."

"Talk," says Ariel. Her voice is not her own. It's part rage, part defeat. Terrell likes the second part.

"At the station. I think we'll be more comfortable there."

Terrell and Boone have debated the merits of interviewing Ariel at the station or in Kristi's office at the gym. The latter offers immediacy. While Ariel is still riled or rattled or whatever she is, Terrell can sweep in and push her to misstep. The office is familiar territory to Ariel though, she may feel comfortable here. That is something Boone and Terrell don't want.

Interviewing Ariel at the police station removes that comfort level. One for the pro side. On the other hand, there will be a delay getting from Vitality+ to the police station. The delay could give Ariel time to regroup and shut down. Or it could add to her discomfort.

It's a coin toss. In this case, the coin landed in favor of the police station. Terrell makes no conversation on the way to the station. Ariel asks no questions and opts for silence. Unfriendly silence. Terrell can feel the tension and her anger. If that's what it is.

Constable Reynolds meets them in the entrance way to the station. He leads Ariel away. Silently. A hand on her elbow and a finger pointing down the hallway.

"How did it go?" Boone asks Terrell watching the constable and the suspect make their way to interrogation room one.

"We'll soon find out."

The Bedford Police Station is one of five community policing stations. Police headquarters are in downtown Halifax. Community stations exist to have a presence in their neighborhoods. That presence comes in two forms: visibility and services. One service is case investigation and closure. Arrests, charges, interrogations, are all done out of the community office.

Regardless what name you put on the building, it is still a police station. The Bedford station looks like a police station, police officers walk in and out of the building, police cars are parked out front, there is a sergeant in full uniform behind the front desk. The sergeant, indeed all the officers, wear guns.

It can be intimidating. That is not what you want when a little girl's bike has been stolen and she is sobbing in your arms. That is exactly what you want when you are trying to bring the weight of the law to bear on someone who has, until now, found that crime does, in fact, pay.

That intimidating atmosphere needs to sink in. As part two of "Ariel under arrest," Terrell and Boone weighed the pros and cons of letting the personal trainer sit in an interrogation room and stew or moving in right away to add to the discomfort she felt spending time with her ex-lover's ex-lover. The former reaffirms who is in control. The latter may prove better timing to trip Ariel up.

Stewing won out. Terrell makes his way to a local coffee shop. He doesn't really want a coffee, but he needs to keep busy. Walking to Java the Hutt takes time, ordering takes time, walking back .... Well, you get it. Terrell orders some organic chocolate espresso thing with a splash of vanilla. He has no idea why.

By the time Terrell gets back to the station, 30 minutes have gone by. He finds Boone and gives her the coffee thing. Then he makes his way to interrogation room one. He sticks his head in the viewing room. Constable Reynolds shakes his head. "Not a word."

"How does she look? Scared to death or fit to be tied?"

"Like a deer in the headlights."

Shellshock is good. Terrell grins and opens the door to the interrogation room. He wipes the grin from his face. Crime is serious business.

"Sorry for the wait. I had trouble reaching the public prosecutor." Terrell hopes that will strike the fear of God further into Ariel even if she doesn't understand what it means. "Prosecutor" is a deer-in-the-headlights word.

Ariel stares at him. "Whatever." Sullen is now setting in. Sullen is not good. It's often followed by defiance. You definitely don't want a defiant suspect. Terrell moves to stamp the sullenness out of his surly suspect.

"I'd suggest you start taking this seriously. Very seriously. Theft – at the level you committed robbery – is an indictable offence."

Ariel stares at him. Terrell raises a hand to stop any potential response. "They like to trot out the word 'indictable' in the legal profession. Think it sounds fancy. What it means is that the feds are now involved. You never want the feds involved. Petty bunch of people."

Ariel stares him. Terrell hasn't been quite honest with Ariel, but that is irrelevant He continues as if they are having a friendly conversation. "So what, you ask? Good question. Pettiness is reflected in the penalties that go along with a crime. In your case, stealing a watch worth more than $5,000, much more, means up to ten years in jail."

Ariel stares at him. This time her jaw drops. "Ahh," Terrell continues. "Another good question. How likely are you to get ten years in jail – federal jail remember. The jail with the bad boys. And girls."

The detective leans in almost like two tweens sharing a dirty joke. "I don't think you'll do ten years. What I know is you will do jail time. My guess, they'll give you two years less a day, which will mean you won't have to be locked up in a federal pen. Not that it matters much. There are no redeeming qualities to being in prison. Any prison."

Ariel starts to open her mouth. Terrell tries not to smile. He has her. He can feel it. She can feel it. Constable Reynolds, breathing more heavily in the earpiece, can feel it. There is a relief in baring one's soul. In confessing. In putting an end to the whole damn thing whatever the damn thing may be.

Terrell reaches for his pen, even though the interview is being recorded. This makes it look official. Reminds criminals that they are just that. Criminals. Ariel starts to cry, a soft sob. That's good. You can speak while sobbing softly. There can be no conversation when someone is bawling, wailing, or blubbering.

Terrell raises his pen.

Ariel opens her mouth.

Boone walks in.

She shoots Terrell a look. He has seen that look before. It is not a good look. "Interview is over."

Terrell's mouth drops. Ariel's mouth drops. Boone would put money on Constable Reynold's mouth dropping. Boone looks directly at Ariel. It is a challenge. "Your lawyer is here."

"I don't have a lawyer," Ariel says obviously confused.

"Are you refusing counsel?" Terrell asks with his last glimmer of hope.

"I said don't have a lawyer, I didn't say I was stupid," Ariel says. Defiantly.

* * *

Lexie watched as Terrell clipped his shield to his waistband. This was it: denouement. Today the case of the missing jewelry would come to an end. At least, that is the hope. Terrell strode through the doorway and stopped. He looked at Ariel looking at Abby looking at him. Lexie looked at the front desk, at Nathan.

If today is a day for taking final steps, Lexie wonders if she, too, should push for a conclusion, a conclusion she knows will be a beginning or an ending. It is the latter fear that stops her from moving forward, literally and figuratively. There is a reason we use band aids: they hide scars; they keep scabs from festering. Lexie's issue is an itch. She has felt it for years and safely ignored it, despite the discomfort. Scratch that itch and she runs the real risk of infection. Flesh-eating disease. Lexie wants to avoid that, but perhaps it can't be avoided.

Terrell has made his way across the gym. He moved with purpose and focus. He moved with ease. This is a man who has pushed for conclusions his entire career. Lexie has pressed for laughs, for being centerstage and visible, until she exits left. Lexie now finds herself following in Terrell's footsteps. When he stopped in front of Ariel, Lexie stopped four feet behind. She felt a hand in hers.

"It's time," says Woo Woo. "You can do this."

Lexie isn't sure she can, but she has come to the conclusion that she has to. She looks at Woo Woo with a wobbly fear. Her friend grips her hand tightly with encouragement, and love. Lexie feels rather than sees Charlene coming up behind them.

"Don't worry," says Woo Woo, "I'll tell her. We'll be in the café."

The front desk, as usual, is clear. There are no coffee mugs, no files, no pens, no brochures of any kind. Lexie wonders why they bother to have a front desk. She makes a mental note to use that in her podcast. Force of habit.

Nathan sees Lexie moving his way. She looks pale and shaky. He hopes everything is okay. He wishes Lexie no ill will. It's his nature. He wonders if it is genetic.

"Hi Nathan." Lexie speaks very softly, uncertain. Nathan nods, encouragement and confusion. "I was wondering if we might start over."

Nathan is more confused now. Lexie sees this. She understands it. "I have not been myself with you, and I fear I may have left an impression I did not want to leave. I am hoping we can get to know each other, the real each other. I thought we could start by starting over."

There is something in Nathan's throat. Unable to speak, he nods. He has been waiting for this moment his whole life. At least, that is what he tells himself. But perhaps that is drama. Nathan wonders if a dramatic nature is inherited.

Lexie understands the importance of delivery. As a comedian, she has learned how critical it is to command the scene, to pave the way for the punchline, to draw the crowd in and keep their attention. She is not going to blow this moment. This is the biggest punchline of her life.

Lexie straightens. She stands tall. She extends her right hand toward Nathan. "Hello. Please let me introduce myself. I am Alexandra Winslow."

Nathan looks at Lexie. He looks at Lexie's hand. He looks at the space between the two of them. He sees the words hanging in the air. *Alexandra Winslow.*

Nathan breaks into tears. Lexie stands still, her hand extended in midair.

Chapter 23.

"No idea," says Boone before Terrell can ask her what the hell is going on. "Some man showed up wearing a $5,000 suit and said he was Ms. Ariel McNichols's lawyer."

"Her last name is McKinley."

"I know that. You know that. Her lawyer, apparently, doesn't know that."

"Someone has hired the lawyer for her."

"Yep. The very expensive lawyer. He's with one of those firms. You know Annoying, Bothersome, More Bothersome, and Arsehole."

"Who has the money and the inclination to keep Ariel McKinley out of jail?"

Boone and Terrell spend the next 20 minutes in her office trying to answer that question. Several people would have the money, Byron Newhouse, for example, but not the inclination. Others, like Nathan Young, might have the inclination but not the cash. It never occurs to either of them it might be Lexie, Charlene, or Woo Woo even though they all have the money and maybe, just maybe, the inclination.

On their second cup of the motor oil the station calls coffee, the question of "who?" is answered. "Why?" remains an enigma. Constable Reynolds appears in the doorway. "Ma'am there is someone here to talk to you and Detective Terrell about the watch and Ms. McKinley. She won't give me her name, but she says there has been a mistake. Says there never was a theft."

The woman standing in the doorway is tall, lithe, manicured, and elegant. She is wearing a taupe coat that Terrell thinks must mimic the hue of newborn camels. He suspects it is just as soft. A scarf, one of those that likely costs more than his biweekly paycheque, is expertly tied around her neck. A splash of color and a reminder that she is from a different world.

Who the hell is she?

As if on cue, tall and elegant walks in, extends her arm. "Sorry to interrupt, and sorry for the subterfuge. I'm Sylvia Newhouse."

It takes Boone and Terrell a few seconds to, metaphorically, pick themselves up off the floor. Sylvia Newhouse waits patiently for them to regain their composure. She is the puppet master here, and she knows exactly what she is doing.

Constable Reynolds returns with a black tea and a slice of lemon. Where the hell did he find lemon? Boone and Terrell shoot him a look. He shrugs. Sylvia Newhouse thanks him and apologizes for the artifice. Terrell thinks he prefers "subterfuge."

She sits down in the chair beside Terrell. Her posture is perfect, but she does not look at all stiff or uncomfortable. She is relaxed and in charge with shoulders back and head high. "I understand there has been some confusion about my husband's watch. The Nautilus 7010."

Message received. There is more than one expensive watch in this household. Boone and Terrell know what they are up against. Doesn't mean they are happy about it – or going to take the subterfuge lying down.

"No confusion at all," says Boone. She is smiling one of those deep smiles that propel the corners of the mouth skyward. Her eyes crinkle. She continues to lean back in her chair as if the three of them are talking about a Michael Bublé concert at the Metro Centre. Her whole demeanor appears to say, "Isn't this delightful." Everyone in the room knows the inspector is really saying, "Screw you."

Sylvia Newhouse is not a woman to be screwed with. She mirrors Boone's smile, sits a little straighter. (Terrell did not think that was possible. He wonders if she does yoga.) Slowly, she sips her tea, reaches into her handbag and passes an envelope to Boone. Before Boone can accept the offering, Sylvia Newhouse tips the envelope upside down. The Nautilus 7010 falls out onto Boone's chipped walnut desk.

"As you can see, my husband's watch is safe and sound."

Boone and Terrell say nothing. That's part tactic, part shock. Either way, it doesn't faze the woman in the camel coat. "I took Byron's watch to replace the battery. He must have forgotten about this, and I didn't realize he had erroneously alerted the police."

Boone takes her time. She sits straighter. She leans forward, like she is sharing a secret with her best friends. She wishes she had a scarf. "To confirm, you walked into Vitality+, went to your husband's locker, removed his watch, and went to the battery store. All without waving at your husband or saying hello to your son."

Sylvia Newhouse leans in. "You got me." She smiles. The corners of her mouth reach heavenward. They drip ice. "I didn't go directly to the battery store."

Tea is served. The kettle has boiled, the selection of herbal, green, chai, and black teas is nicely spread on a decorative plate. Lexie is very pleased with the plate. She got it at the Dollar Store. There is an assortment of cheese, crackers, fruit, muffins, and cookies. Indeed, there is enough food for a small army. Lexie hopes everyone is hungry.

Kristi is coming at 2:30. Lexie expects her friends to arrive well before then. In part, it will be to discuss strategy. Mostly though her friends will come early because they are worried about her. Lexie feels her eyes well up. She is so blessed to have friends.

The Nathan situation is just that, Nathan's situation. Lexie has put it out there; the next step is up to her son.

Charlene and Woo Woo drive to Lexie's together. They are worried about their friend. They aren't sure how to transform this worry into action, or if they should. They understand this is about supporting their friend, but it's been a while since they have had a friend to support. Both are concerned about making a misstep, about making things worse.

Lexie knows all this at some level. What she knows even more is people care about her. That makes things better. It has been a while since things have felt better. She opens the door and hugs her friends. Enough said.

There is a perfunctory discussion about Kristi and the best approach. Everyone agrees on what they have already agreed to. Woo Woo places her hand on top of Lexie's. Charlene would like to swat it away. Lexie shoots her a grin.

Kristi is on time. She's looking forward to tea with her new friends. She feels on the fringe of this friendship. The fringe will do. Kristi wants to talk about what happened this morning. She saw the detective leave with Ariel. Have they heard from Terrell? They have not. Did they expect to? Maybe.

Lexie is looking with some suspicion at the green liquid in her cup. It looks remarkably like vomit.

"Matcha," Woo Woo says by way of explanation. "I brought some with me. It's good for you." She pushes the cup closer to Lexie's mouth. Lexie sips. Woo Woo grins.

Charlene turns to Kristi. "We have an idea we'd like to discuss with you." So much for the plan.

The ulterior motive for tea does not seem to surprise Kristi. The idea does.

Daily Thoughts – Woo Woo
Saturday, October 26th

I need this, need you, today. Need to collect my thoughts, put them on paper, and see what I am thinking. For the most part, I am feeling. Most of me, frankly, is reeling. So much has happened, much of it good. Perhaps all of it is good. Perhaps not. I need to separate the emotion from the actual. It's a meditation thing. But you know that.

Everything went well with Kristi. That's a plus, for everyone. Our cool, calm, collected auditor waited all of twelve minutes before she blurted out that we had something we wanted to discuss with Kristi. Lexie and I laughed about it afterwards. I swear Charlene blushed. At the time though, our jaws dropped.

It didn't seem to matter, and maybe it helped. I have the feeling Kristi knew something was up, but she also knows we care about her. Our offer would only reinforce that. I think Kristi is grateful and appreciative. She is also cautious. Who wouldn't be? Her former partner stole from her and treated her like last week's leftovers. Now she will have three partners with different personalities and different approaches to operating a business. She has my sympathy.

Charlene is quite keen on this. I think she's really looking forward to running a company with friends. I'm looking forward to having friends who will run a company together. See the difference. I know it's semantics and I know it's nuance, but I don't want Lexie or Charlene to be disappointed. Or Kristi. The lawyers can protect Kristi. You can't protect how we'll feel if the friendship falls apart. Please, don't fall apart.

Part of me thinks I should tell my dad. He'll be thrilled I'm going into business. He does not think reflexology is a business. I will debate that with him, but he is right. We both know it. I love my dad, and I love that he will want to help. I think for now though, I need to do this on my own. It's not like my trust fund is running low. I have enough money to buy several gyms. In several countries. Simultaneously.

It's not about money then, this urge to pick up the phone and yell, "Daddy, guess what?" It's not about Daddy's approval. I have that. I think it's about letting my father know I am okay. I am going to continue to be okay. I have great friends.

I will give my dad a complimentary membership. That will be the first thing I do when I am the co-owner of Vitality+. I can't wait.

Lexie is doing well, I think. She was present during our meeting with Kristi. She laughed. She told jokes. She didn't look sad. She also didn't tell Kristi about Nathan. She will. Not now though. Now is the time to let things be. She has put it out to the universe. The universe, of course, is Nathan. What Nathan will do with this, no one knows. Probably not even Nathan. He may have suspected, but that isn't the same as knowing. Now he knows.

I wonder if Lexie had a dream of what might be for the two of them. Or what should not be. I sense she has stopped dreaming. I think that is a good thing. Let the universe work its magic. Maybe the magic has already happened. Maybe getting it out there into the world is enough. It seems to be enough for Lexie. For now.

It's interesting how a few hours change how you see the world. How you feel about that world. I have gone from worrying about my friend Lexie to worrying about Michael, my .... Who knows? Worry isn't the right word. Michael is a seasoned detective. (*Seasoned.* I must have read that somewhere.) He will find perspective over the watch and the people who upended his case. He knows who two of them are. I mean they were in the station with him. He seems to be struggling to figure out the third person.

That surprises me. Seasoned as he is and all, Charlene, Lexie, and I knew who it was within seconds of him telling us the story. The issue for us is what to do with what we know. We didn't have a chance to discuss it, Michael and Kristi were both there. I'll call the girls first thing tomorrow.

I think there is something we could do.

Sincerely,

Shondra Aeron

Chapter 24.

The sun has been up for at least an hour. Christian watched it rise. It is a clear day, and the rays spread gently from the east through the grove of trees at the end of his street to the kid on the skateboard to his bedroom. Christian basked in that glow. Bask is the wrong word. It implies a savoring, a luxuriating. Christian just sat. And let life eat at him like the sun eats shadows.

He knows the sun rises in the east each day (at least until some scientist proves otherwise). He thought he had that same reliability in his life. Parents. School. Jade. Now he's not sure. About any of it.

On the surface, he still has his parents and school. He is leery to dig beneath that surface but knows it must be done. He's not sure when it should be done. Perhaps a decade from now. He would like that.

Christian knows digging beneath the surface will not wait a decade. It has barely waited for the sun to rise. The landscape with the fewest landmines is school. Christian hates it. Always has. He does not want an advanced degree in business. He does not want an empire. That is what his father wants. Pleasing his father was easy when he had Jade. They met for lunch. Grabbed coffee when they needed a break. Caught up with each other at the end of the day. Those were wonderful days. School was more than bearable; it was a special place. Their place. A place where Byron and Sylvia Newhouse did not deign to go.

Past tense. Christian is aware he is thinking in the past tense, awareness what was is no longer. Jade is gone. His parents are not. If he quits school, there will be histrionics. Most of them his father's. His mother will chime in. She would like to introduce her son as Dr. Newhouse. That carries with it a risk though. Someone might ask what kind of medicine he practices, and his mother will have to admit he has a PhD. Somewhat akin to lice. At least in this context, and his mother would have played out all the contexts in her mind.

That leaves continuing with school. Dragging his reluctant body to a beige room every day to explore the wonders of the talent cliff. Focus groups. Surveys. Literature searches. Thesis defense. Christian would like to jump off a cliff.

Completing his doctorate also means going to school, where Jade goes. What if he runs into her? What will he say? Christian's biggest fear is he will say nothing. Do nothing. Go back to the beige room and cry.

He tries to take Jade out of the equation. Christian has had his heart broken before. He knows it will heal, although with Jade it will be forever scarred. Picture this: Christian on the podium, accepting his PhD, touching the tassel on his left side. Turning to look out at the audience. Seeing his parents in the front row. Beaming. He feels their pride. He feels his sense of accomplishment. He feels the heat of joy radiating through his body.

Nope. That is the morning sun. Christian moves into the shadow. There is no beaming, no pride, no euphoria. No Jade. Christian knows what he must do.

He is less certain what is going on with his parents and whether there is anything he can do, or should. When his mother got home yesterday, she was glowing. He hadn't seen her this happy in a long time. Finally, Christian remembers thinking, something is going right.

As supper approached, his mother's mood actually improved. He swears he heard her singing a Taylor Swift song as she marinated a pork roast and peeled potatoes. That domesticity, in and of itself, was unusual. Dinner was typically take-out and on your own.

"I'm making a sit-down meal for us tonight," Sylvia had said with some delight. "It will be a wonderful family dinner."

What Sylvia meant was a wonderful dinner for her. When Byron got home shortly after 6:30, he was as surprised as Christian by this happy, bouncing woman impersonating his wife. Byron had the good sense to be suspicious.

Dinner went well. Sylvia was full of conversation and anecdotes about her day. She asked, solicitously, after her family and their day. The pork roast was tender and moist, the potatoes whipped into buttery submission, and the vegetables lightly salted and deliciously fresh.

"Wait until you see what we're having for dessert."

Christian should have been on full alert. He was too sated. Byron was also starting to drop his guard. Sylvia made her way into the kitchen and returned with ice cream – Häagen-Dazs mango raspberry. Byron dished up heaping bowls for all of them. He was smiling. Sylvia leaned in as Byron brought the first spoonful to his lips.

"You forgot the cherry on top." She brought out an envelope, looked her husband in the eyes. Any pretense of conviviality was gone. Sylvia flipped the envelope upside down. A Patek Philippe fell out.

Byron jumped back as if scalded. "What the hell is this?"

"This is your watch, dear." Christian will never forget the sound of his mother's voice.

Christian replays the prelude to dinner, the meal, the finale in his mind. Then he replays it again. He wonders if perhaps it is just as well he and Jade are over. Yesterday with his family, and most of the days before that, are not what he wants in life. He wants family, but he wants security, and joy, and the knowledge he is loved unconditionally.

His parents must have had that at some point. They clearly don't have it now. He is not sure why they stay together although he suspects it has to do with money and status. Would he and Jade have clung to things other than each other? He thinks not, but there are no certainties in life.

He is not certain whether his father will ever forgive his mother. He is not certain whether his mother will ever stop singing that damn song.

Christian knows what he must do.

* * *

It is too early to have worked up a large appetite, but Terrell is tearing into his eggs benedict like he has not ever seen food before. He knows this is transference. Cops learn that in rookie training, along with CPR and de-escalation. It is usually a reference to witnesses, sometimes CIs and even accused, leaning more heavily on an officer than is healthy, transferring their anger, fear, and remorse to the warm, breathing human in front of them.

Terrell is transferring his pent-up emotions to soft-poached eggs that are getting a little cold and hollandaise sauce that is starting to congeal. What he is not doing is carrying on a conversation with Boone, his boss and breakfast mate. Conversation is conveniently difficult thanks to mouthfuls of egg etcetera. In keeping with his uninterrupted breakfast-plate concentration, Terrell is also not looking at the inspector sitting a few feet from him.

Boone knows exactly what is going on. There is a discussion that needs to be had. Neither of them want to have it. There are a number of reasons for their mutual reluctance. Topping the list is embarrassment. The Halifax Police Department, specifically Michael Terrell and Jennifer Boone, has been played. It is not a nice feeling and no amount of peameal bacon will fill the void or diminish the anger.

There is also the outstanding question of who the hell played them. Terrell and Boone have been over this individually and repeatedly in their minds. They have suspects, and they are about to lay those suspects out, metaphorically at least, on the well-aged oak table that also holds two cups of steaming coffee and now the remnants of two eggs benny.

"It certainly wasn't Newhouse," says Terrell. "I don't think for a moment he loved Ariel and rushed in to rescue her like a knight in shining armor."

"Even if chivalry is alive and well, he wouldn't rescue his paramour by calling on his wife to help. I imagine she's furious. Sylvia Newhouse does not strike me as a woman who forgets and forgives."

"Then there is some justice. I would like to see Newhouse pay in some small way for all this crap he brought on himself – and us."

Terrell and Boone rule out Christian next. He would have access to a lawyer, but it's unlikely he knew about his father's affair or knew Ariel well enough to find out where she hid the watch. Likewise, there is little reason to suspect Sylvia Newhouse knew about the affair or cared if she did. And why would a wife rush to the defense of her husband's lover, even if she isn't fond of said husband.

Potentially Ariel could have blackmailed Sylvia to come to her rescue, although Terrell and Boone are stumped as to what that blackmail could have been or how Ariel could have reached out to Sylvia between being detained and having her lawyer walk in the interrogation room. Ariel did not make any phone calls.

Abby also ends up on the cutting room floor as a suspect. She might like to get back at Newhouse, but then, she already has. And why would she help Ariel? Or engage her ex-lover's wife as a co-conspirator? No, Abby Downton is looking out for Abby Downton, not Ariel McKinley.

Joining Abby on the cutting room floor is Kristi Yee. No motive, no opportunity, no money. That leaves, uncomfortably,

Charlie's Angels. Lexie, Charlene, and Woo Woo have the money and the means to hire a lawyer. They have the acumen to get that lawyer to the police station. They even have the smarts to figure out where the watch is. The question is why?

"There is nothing in this for them even taking into account any desire to be 'nice,'" says Boone.

For Terrell, this is about more than means, motive, and opportunity. It's personal. In one case, it may be deeply personal. But Terrell thinks like a cop. It's the only way to identify likely suspects – and rule out others. "They might not want to see Ariel go to jail, especially for a man like Newhouse. We both know, if convicted, McKinley would do jail time. It wouldn't be pretty."

"The problem here is no one expected to like the thief better than the victim. At the very least, no one wants to see a young woman go to prison because she got conned by a letch."

As much as he hates to admit it, Terrell could see the three amigos rushing in to Ariel's defense. Boone agrees, but she has a caveat. "I have no doubt those three women would insert themselves into this part of the investigation to save Ariel. Crap, I can see them flying in through the door of the interrogation room yelling, 'Halt.' What I cannot see is them, any of them, doing that to you."

Terrell hopes his boss is right.

* * *

Woo Woo has been tapped to call Ariel's avenging angel. She tries to keep things neutral, not an easy task for Woo Woo. She does okay. They have an appointment for later that afternoon.

Lexie, Charlene, and Woo Woo are conclaving over coffee. Well, it's really green tea and pumpkin spiced lattes. (Charlene has bought a new Saeco coffee maker, at least new to her.) Two issues: how to handle the avenging angel and how to let Terrell know what they are doing. More correctly, what they have done.

That appears to be the easy decision. Woo Woo invites Terrell and Boone over that evening for munchies and a glass of wine or a cold beer. "We wanted to catch you up," she texts.

While they are waiting for a reply, they return to where the conversation started. "I think we just dive in and hope for the best," Charlene says. "It worked well with Kristi." Woo Woo and Lexie give her a look. She tries not to blush.

"We know Kristi," Lexie points out. "We have no idea how this person will react."

That is the wrinkle in every option. Reveal your hand too soon and be shown to the door. Take too much time to put your cards on the table and that is time for your opponent to come up with an out or an alternative plan.

"Do you really think they are an 'opponent'?" Woo Woo asks.

"Who knows?" says Charlene. "What we know about this person fits on one page, double spaced."

The buzzer sounds to let the three women in. Woo Woo takes it as a good sign they are welcomed in so quickly. Charlene thinks there is no other choice but to buzz them in. Lexie wonders if she should bring a munchie to Woo Woo's tonight.

The front door is open when the women arrive at #716. Lexie sticks her head inside and yells, "Hello."

"Make yourselves comfortable," a voice replies from somewhere inside. "I'm making us some drinks."

Woo Woo, Lexie, and Charlene walk inside and head for the living room, straight ahead. They each take a chair. Lexie leans forward and picks up the book on the coffee table. *The Thong Principle*. "This should be fun."

Abby Downton comes into the living room a few minutes later. She is holding a tray of mojitos. "Thought we might as well make a good time of this."

Well, the planning was a waste, Charlene thinks. This woman is one step ahead of us. It also explains why she was one step ahead of the police.

"So, you've bought Vitality+," Abby says. "That seems like a sound investment."

"We've bought into Vitality+," Charlene corrects her. "We're partners with Kristi Yee, one of the original owners."

"Does Ariel still have a job?"

"She does," Lexie says. "Kristi felt there was no reason to let her go. Bad judgment, good trainer. Unlikely to make the same mistake twice."

"Byron is a mistake," agrees Abby.

"We're friends with Michael Terrell," Woo Woo says. It comes out in a rush, and unexpectedly. She wonders if she is sharing Charlene's aura.

"Ahh," says Abby. She takes a long sip of her drink. "He's a looker." Woo Woo turns a deep shade of magenta. Abby laughs.

"What can I do for you?"

"We wanted to tie up the loose ends for Terrell and his boss," says Charlene. "We thought it only right."

Abby considers this implicit request and its implications. "Are the police pressing charges?"

"Not as far as we know," says Charlene. "What could they charge anyone with? There has been no crime."

"You and I know there has been a crime," Abby says. "The police know it too."

"Their hands are tied," says Lexie. "No one is admitting to a theft. Just the reverse. And no one is out any money except, of course, the police."

Abby rises from her chair. She nods at the women. "I forgot the cheese and crackers. Thought we might work up an appetite."

Charlene and Lexie see this for what it is. A stall tactic. Abby has bought herself some time to consider her options. Woo Woo thinks it was very nice of Abby to give them a little something to eat.

Eating a few pieces of cheese and crackers buys Abby a little more time. It is time she doesn't need. "Here's the deal. I'll answer your questions, and you are free to share that info with the detective and his boss on one condition. You confirm first that no charges will be laid. Unless they are charging Byron. I'm okay with that."

Boone is intrigued. This is her first invitation to meet with the triad. She is not quite sure what to expect, except she knows it will be eye-opening. It has been so far. Terrell hasn't told her much except she will be surprised. She already knew that.

The two officers are travelling together. Terrell knows where he is going, they live quite close to one another, it's good for the environment. Mostly though, Terrell wants to see the look on Boone's face when they pull up in front of Woo Woo's house.

It's everything he thought it would be and then some. Slack-jawed. Big-eyed. Boone's head goes back, her breath rushes out in a single "oof." But she didn't make inspector for her good looks. It takes her only a second to realize she has been had. "Sonofabitch."

Terrell takes the name calling good naturedly. Once he stops laughing. "Her father owns Aeron Aerospace."

The set-up gave Terrell a good laugh. More importantly, it gave Boone a chance to reset her face. That bland, blasé look cops are trained to wear like a second skin. This is important to Terrell because he knows it is important to Woo Woo that money not be something that sets her apart or draws people to her.

By the time they ring the front bell, which Boone swears sounds like the chiming of Westminster Abbey, the inspector is composed, nonchalant even. Woo Woo welcomes them in like long lost friends. She is so glad they've come. One of them in particular.

The three friends agreed they would all make something for tonight. Put a little effort into the evening. Woo Woo has prepared apple nachos with pumpkin caramel. It's really a dessert, and it's really vegan, but she's not telling anyone this. Charlene went old school with devilled eggs, and Lexie whipped up some Swedish meatballs. Actually, she took some Swedish meatballs out of her freezer, but they were ones she had made herself. There is also cheese and crackers to go with the wine and some sliders for the beer drinkers.

"I may come more often," says Boone looking over the array. She accepts a glass of sauvignon blanc from Lexie and sits down. Madoff promptly jumps in her lap. This is a big night for Madoff. He usually gets left at home. And he doesn't know this person. She may have treats. Boone looks into Madoff's brown eyes and gives his left ear a scratch. She is rewarded with a furry cheek against her chest. "Yes, I will definitely come more often."

The women are pleased with how well the evening is going, although if Charlene is being honest with herself nothing has "gone" so far. There has been no discussion, only a few pleasantries. Everyone is waiting for the opening salvo, or the axe to fall.

Terrell brings them back to business. "Aside from learning we like beer, wine, and Charlene's dog (Madoff looks up. Boone swears he smiled), I'm assuming there is something you want to share with us."

The three women look at each other. They drew straws to determine who would lead the discussion. Lexie lost. Or won, depending on your point of view. Lexie shares the process with Terrell and Boone. She wants them to know this was not easy for her and her friends, and that the intent is to be helpful, not nosy. Well, a little nosy.

Terrell and Boone wait for Lexie to get to the point. There is no rush. Cops are trained to wait. Then wait some more. And this is much better than a car with c-store snacks and a bottle for a bathroom. Lexie sets the scene: stolen watch, Ariel the thief, recovered watch, Ariel the innocent. Boone scoffs at this interpretation. Lexie gives her a grin. "None of us is buying that, so the question is how did Ariel go from criminal to victim. We know the answer."

Terrell quietly takes a sip of beer. He can feel the stillness in his body. He wonders if this is what meditation feels like. Boone sits forward. Madoff eats the meatball she is absently feeding him.

"Would you like to guess?" Woo Woo asks. Woo Woo knows she isn't supposed to say anything, but she feels the tension, and she likes games.

Boone bursts out laughing, and the moment passes from friction to familiarity. The inspector turns to Terrell. "Twenty buck says it's Sylvia's son Christian. Only thing that would make that woman help her husband's ex-lover is her son."

Terrell nods. So, they are doing this. "It's not Christian. It's Abby."

Woo Woo beams. Charlene claps. Lexie grins. Madoff licks Boone so she doesn't feel so bad. There were also a few crumbs in her lap.

Once the culprit is confirmed, there are few surprises. Abby wanted to get even with Newhouse. She didn't want another woman to suffer at his indifferent and arrogant hands. She certainly didn't want another woman to go to jail for trying to get back at the lying S-O-B. She also wanted to stick it to him, and what better way than to involve his wife.

That's the part that confuses Terrell. Why would Sylvia Newhouse help her husband's lovers? Plural. (Hint: Read the previous paragraph.)

There is also the question of timing. Abby assured her guests over several mojitos that this little plan of hers was spur of the moment. She had been enjoying keeping Ariel on tenterhooks, but when she saw Terrell come out of yoga class, the reality of what was about to happen hit home. This woman, this almost kid, was going to jail for a watch she didn't even want.

According to Abby's version of events, she called Sylvia Newhouse to explain the situation and asked Sylvia to help. Sylvia had been reluctant to get involved. She didn't like any of the players in this theatre of the absurd although she was enamored of the idea of sticking it to her husband. Abby convinced her to send a lawyer to the police station while she was contemplating taking on the role of director. Sylvia agreed.

"That leaves only how they got the watch," Terrell says.

"That was much easier than it would appear, and all legal," says Charlene. "Ariel's lawyer asked her where it was, and he told Sylvia."

"And where was it?" Boone asks. "We looked everywhere — including her apartment and her car once we got a search warrant.”

“It was taped to the underside of one of the treadmills in the gym,” says Lexie.

“We searched that gym thoroughly,” says Terrell. There is a hint of defensiveness.

“We said the same thing,” says Charlene. “While you were searching the gym, Ariel had the watch around her ankle.”

“Clever girl,” says Woo Woo. She forgot to read the room.

Daily Thoughts – Charlene
Sunday, October 26th

It's 2 a.m. Perhaps that makes it October 27th. Not that it matters. What's one more day when your father is a philanderer. So, apparently, I am jumping right in. It is very un-auditor like. I take comfort in process. If the process takes time, so be it. The process, of course, needs to be tried and true. Evidently, I am into cliches in the early morning hours.

Truth is I'm inspired by Lexie. And I am scared to death. Well, not death. But scared. This is foreign territory for me. I do not know where the IEDs are buried. (Watched *Seal Team* an hour ago.) Dora wouldn't care. She'd just barrell across the terrain without a second's thought. If something blows up, it blows up. Woo Woo would say it was meant to be. Perhaps they are both right.

I don't like being wrong, and I don't like this feeling of walking on a marshmallow. Now I'm hungry.

Took a quick break. Made myself a hot chocolate with mallows. It's delicious. I won't sleep, of course, but I wasn't going to anyway. My absence does not appear to bother Madoff. Just as well. No point in both of us being out of sorts.

This man who says he is my half-brother. Repeatedly says he is my half-brother. Why won't he let this go?

His name is Sam. Short for Samuel. My father had a brother Samuel. I never met him. He died in the second world war. Lied about his age and enlisted. Too young to know better.

Then again Sam is a common name. Almost everyone has a brother, uncle, nephew, daughter named Sam. Doesn't make us blood relatives. Nor does some online DNA testing company that also contends I'm eight percent African.

Sam lives in Ottawa. A tidbit in one of the many email/phone messages he has left. Dad worked in Ottawa a lot. Government bureaucrats usually do. Doesn't mean they're procreating while they are project managing.

I know my father. He was a decent man. Honest. Ethical. Fair. He wouldn't do anything like this as a fling. Would he do it if he fell in love? I don't know.

Does it matter? There is this man who says my blood and his share the DNA of the person I loved the most in this world. I do not want to share my DNA. Dora would be thrilled to know there were other Kurtzes out there, Kurtzes with a story outside the mainstream. My mother would be mortified if she were still alive. But she would forgive my father anything, even this. I will follow in her footsteps.

Forgiveness is one thing. Embracing the little sod is another. Would my mother do that? Dora will bake him a friggin' cake. She will be intolerable. Her Christmas gift to me has spawned this gift, the greatest gift of all, family and love. Lord spare me.

So, two pages in and I am no further ahead. I'm here at this ungodly hour because Lexie has inspired me. She goes to university as a kid, gets pregnant, gives up said kid, and thirty years later she is looking that kid squarely in the face and introducing herself. Come what may.

I am not a come-what-may kinda gal. I'm not sure Lexie is either. Even if I'm not, doesn't mean I couldn't be.

I poked Madoff. He is not happy. He was snug as a bug. Now he is downstairs with me wrapped in a blanket unsure why he had to be displaced. I'm not either. Yet here we are.

I'll wrap up. Ariel is not going to jail. In fact, Ariel is going to keep working at Vitality+. Terrell and Boone are pissed. Woo Woo is fretting she offended the beau. Lexie has found some compartment, somewhere in the inner workings of her mind, where she has gently placed her son. All of the aforementioned, I assume, are sleeping soundly in their beds. I am here massaging Madoff's back with some glove dogs are supposed to love. Madoff does not love the glove.

I need to resolve this. I need to resolve it now. If only for Madoff's sake.

Sincerely,

Charlene Kurtz

Chapter 25.

The early morning sun glints off the Bedford Basin. It bathes the Asana Yoga Studio in warmth and light. The oak floors gleam in the glow. A bronze frog in full lotus smiles. In the empty room, there is stillness and serenity.

Kristi Yee is about to break the tranquility as she does most mornings of her life. The yoga instructor opens the double doors and steps inside. Quietly and respectfully. She takes a minute to breathe in peace, exhale gratitude. It is her morning ritual. This morning, she is very grateful. For her practice, for her studio, for friends who have helped to save this studio and the gym in which it lives.

Within a few minutes, yogis begin to arrive. Charlene and Lexie are first, coming in the door together laughing. Woo Woo is right behind them. She must have stopped to say hello to someone. Woo Woo is always stopping to say hello to someone. Bonnie and Archina enter as if on cue. Honey soon after. Bhodi strolls in with a few minutes to spare. Time enough to warm up with an audience. The final two students arrive as

Kristi is lowering the lights and beginning the music. Terrell and Boone grab a spot at the back of the studio, unroll their mats, and apologize quietly. They are assured all is good. Boone swears the frog winked at her.

Kristi begins with the breath, helping her yogis inhale and exhale in ways that expand both body and spirit. She moves them into a series of twists designed to move the spine in the six ways a healthy spine needs to move. This is routine for the regulars. Terrell and Boone seem relaxed, keeping pace. Feeling like you belong is critical to coming back to class Kristi has learned.

Indeed, Boone is thinking there is nothing to this yoga stuff. She expected more of a challenge. Terrell knows what is coming. He can't wait. He turns to the left in his half lord of the fishes pose and grins at his boss.

The group moves from the mat to a standing position. Kristi takes them to the wall in preparation for bird of paradise. First the group does tree pose. Several people have their foot resting on their inner thigh. Most have it on their calf. Boone tries to get her foot above her knee. It refuses. No one falls over.

They move from the wall to the middle of the mat. Tree pose is repeated. This time the room shimmies and shakes with wobbling bodies trying to find their balance. Kristi reminds them to focus, to stare at something and hold their gaze. "Find your drishti. And breathe."

Bonnie realizes her jaw is clamped shut. She relaxes. Her tree straightens. She gives her inner self a smile. Bhodi is ramrod straight. A mighty oak. The mighty oak stumbles, however. Bhodi took his eye off his drishti to see how many people were admiring his pose. The answer is none, although Woo Woo is trying to hold back a grin. The effort makes her right leg teeter. Karma.

More difficult poses follow: archer, bound triangle, extended head to toe. Boone shoots Terrell a look. It is the same look that has made hardened criminals confess. He looks chagrined. Mostly grinned.

Finally, pose of the week. Bird of paradise is an advanced pose. Svarga dvijasana. Kristi reminds everyone it is not about doing the pose to perfection, it is about your edge. Find your edge and breathe. No pain, no gain is not a mantra yogis use. It's one they refute.

Woo Woo is standing upright. Her left leg pointed toward the ceiling. Her hands clasp her thigh. She is breathing evenly, calmly. Lexie thinks she actually looks like a bird of paradise flower. Charlene thinks she is annoying. Terrell can't take his eyes off her.

Now it's time for savasana. The yogis lie back, sore, hot, content. Boone thinks she may never get up again. Kristi comes by each person, quietly, respectfully, and places a blanket beneath their head. The blanket is infused with lemon and black spruce. Boone thinks she will come back tomorrow.

Several hands go up. There will be a good crowd for coffee. Charlene and Lexie head down to claim a spot. Bonnie and Archina have their heads buried in the savasana blankets. Woo Woo helps Kristi clear away the remaining props. She feels a co-owner should do this.

Terrell and Boone head out the door. Terrell thinks she just called him a bastard, but he is distracted. Ariel is standing behind the front desk. It looks like she is smirking, but he is several yards away. Boone realizes her profanity has been wasted on her friend. She follows his gaze. "Might as well do it now and get it over with."

Ariel sees the dynamic duo heading her way. She stiffens. There are several uncomfortable seconds of silence when Terrell and Boone arrive at the front desk. This is deliberate on the part of the two police detectives. It is inexperience on Ariel's part.

"We would normally do this while we are officially on duty, but since you're here and we're here...."

Ariel waits for Boone to finish. The inspector admires her control. Terrell wonders if this is fear shutting her down or self-protection. "We'd like to officially inform you that the Halifax Police

Department will not be pressing any charges against you. The case is now closed."

Terrell keeps his eyes on Ariel. She looks back at him, then Boone. She smirks. So not fear, Terrell thinks to himself.

Boone leans in. She grips the front of the desk with both hands. She doesn't take her eyes off Ariel. "The case is closed now. It can be re-opened. There are enough holes in your story to drive a tank through. And I know. I drove a Leo for three years in Afghanistan. I can disarm an IED at 700 meters without stopping. I can take you down in split seconds."

Ariel is no longer smirking. Boone is. The inspector turns and walks away. Confidently. Terrell is by her side. "I didn't know you drove an army tank."

"I didn't. That would be my sister. I'm the delicate flower in the family."

As Terrell and Boone cross the gym floor, the front doors open. Christian and Jade stroll through. Terrell tries to hide his surprise, and his delight, at seeing them together. He wasn't sure that would happen. Before he can say anything, Christian walks forward and extends his hand. Terrell, still masking surprise, accepts the offer.

"Thank you," Christian says.

"You're welcome." Terrell means it. He is not sure how he has helped but there has been a shift in this man. His stance is steadier, his gaze direct, his voice clear.

Christian turns to Boone. "I'm not sure we've met. I'm Christian Newhouse. This is my fiancé, Jade Dhillon."

* * *

The café is crowded. Charlene and Lexie pushed three tables together to accommodate the bigger group. Woo Woo also purchased a plate of muffins as a treat for everyone. There is a sense of fun and familiarity. Everyone is comfortable, and the conversation is easy. There is no talk of missing watches or unexpected items falling from yoga mats. Instead, the discussion has turned to football and soccer and what is the correct term. Archina seems quite firm on this.

Lexie is reaching for a second muffin – what? she worked hard this morning – when she feels two hands on her thighs. Woo Woo and Charlene squeeze. Lexie looks up. Nathan is standing at the end of the large, makeshift table. Everyone looks at him. He is only looking at Lexie. "Would you mind if I join you?"

Boone shoots Terrell a questioning look. She can read a room. She can't quite read what is going on here. Terrell places his hand on hers. Woo Woo and Charlene silently squeeze a thigh. Lexie is not sure she can

298

speak. She nods. She opens her mouth. "Please."

Charlene looks at her friend. She can't imagine what is going through her mind, what is happening to her body, what her spirit is feeling. But she knows this. Her friend took a risk and today, in this place at this moment, it has paid off. It might all fall apart tomorrow, or next week or next year. Right now, there is joy. And even if it all goes to bat shit, there is resilience in this woman. This woman who has two friends who instinctively squeezed her thighs.

There is a momentary shuffle to make room for the new addition. Before anyone can grab another chair, Charlene stands up. "Here, take mine. I have a call to make."

The natural rhythm of friends and acquaintances enjoying each other's company resumes. The conversation moves from soccer to the best eggs benny in the city. Bonnie is quite firm on this. She has a favorite diner in Dartmouth. Kevin writes the name down. Nathan smiles at the table, at his life. Lexie looks at her son and tries to hold back tears. Woo Woo beams at the whole table.

Honey farts.

The End

Donalee Moulton books also published by BWL Publishing Inc.

Hung Out to Die

donalee Moulton is an award-winning freelance journalist who has written for print and online publications across North America including *The Globe and Mail, Chatelaine, Lawyer's Daily,* and the *National Post. Bind* is her second mystery book. Her short story "Swan Song" was one of 21 selected for publication in *Cold Canadian Crime* and a second short story has been published in *Black Cat Weekly.* donalee is the author of *Conflagration,* an historical novel set in 1734 Quebec, and is also the author of *The Thong Principle: Saying What You Mean and Meaning What You Say* and co-author of *Celebrity Court Cases.*

donalee Moulton books also published by BWL Publishing

Hung Out to Die

www.ingramcontent.com/pod-product-compliance
Lightning Source LLC
Chambersburg PA
CBHW070113120726
47909CB00002B/583